THE DRAGUNOV SOLUTION

By

Craig Roberts

The Dragunov Solution   2

Consolidated Press International
Tulsa, Oklahoma

ISBN 13: 978-1495223570

ISBN 10: 1495223574

First CPI Printing January 2014

10 9 8 7 6 5 4 3 2 1

"Ship me somewheres east of Suez, where the best
is like the worst,
Where there aren't no Ten Commandments and a
man can raise a thirst;

For the temple-bells are callin', and it's there that I
would be-By the old Moulmein Pagoda, looking
lazy at the sea."

Rudyard Kipling

Mandalay

This book is dedicated to the survivors:
Those of us who were there,
and
Those at home who supported us.

It is also dedicated to those whose names
will remain with us forever, on The Wall.

PROLOGUE

July 1956.
The village of Ho Nam Khe, North Vietnam.

"Note how the heel is deeper than the toe," said Uncle Quan as he pointed at the footprint in the ground. "This means that the man was not worried about noise when he walked. Can you tell me how I know that he was walking and not running?"

"Yes uncle. It is because his foot prints are not far apart." Young Nguyen Van Truong was a very attentive student of the woodcraft that Uncle Quan taught. "How can you tell that he did not care about noise?"

"A man who is moving silently will put equal weight on his foot slowly to test the ground before moving forward, or even put his weight on his toes, letting the front of his foot bear his weight before his heel touches the ground. A man who is careless is easy to track."

"But what if he is being careful and you lose his tracks?"

Uncle Quan smiled. "A good tracker never loses the track of his quarry. Watch!" Quan moved off the trail and studied the vegetation. Selecting a small sapling, he drew his machete and cut it off near the base. Quickly stripping the twigs from its bark, he cut it to length. He then took the five foot staff and lay it upon the ground with the large end touching the heel of the foot print. He then carved a notch where it touched the tip of the toe. After this he slowly moved the opposite tip in an arc until it touched the back of the heel of the next foot print. Again he carved a notch.

"See? This is the stride. I can now lay the staff in the heel of the next foot print and by slowly moving the tip across the ground, have a reference where the next foot print should be. If the man starts running, the next print will be farther away. If that happens, I will make a second mark in the stick for a running stride." Quan watched Truong's face for the look of enlightenment.

"But Uncle Quan, what if the ground is very hard?"

"Where a man or animal goes, he leaves his sign." Moving ahead, they located a patch of hard ground where the footprints seemingly disappeared. Here Uncle Quan produced a small pocket mirror. Holding it at an angle near the ground, he caught the rays of the sun and played the reflection across the surface. Quickly a shadow appeared on the edge of a slight depression, marking what had been an invisible print.

"Look at the blades of grass on the edge of the print. See how they bend forward?"

Young Truong knelt and studied the grass. "Yes, Uncle. What does that mean?"

"That is the direction the man is moving. If he tries to fool you by walking backwards, the grass will be bent in that direction." Quan stood and looked down the hill. "Come with me and see what happens next."

At the base of the hill was a dry stream bed, hard with flat rock. Stopping there, Quan squatted as if to rest. "If a man tries to lose a tracker, he may think he is safe when he finds a hard surface such as this. A good tracker will know what to look for."

Quan and Truong walked twenty meters up the stream bed and stopped. Quan then turned and carefully walked back to where they began, avoiding the same path.

"Look." Quan squatted and pointed at the rock. Truong could see nothing unusual.

"I do not see, Uncle Quan."

"Look closer. See the little pebbles that have been moved, leaving slight marks on the rock where they have scratched the surface?"

"Ah, yes!" Truong could then see the slight scratches where the small stones had scooted from being stepped on.

"Follow the mark from the beginning to the resting place of the pebble, and that is the direction the man moved!" Uncle Quan stood and turned toward the trail back to the village.

"Enough for one day. It is time for you to study your school work now. It is not enough to know the ways of the forest these days."

The eight-year-old boy caught up with his uncle and walked quickly at his side to keep up. "Will you tell me more of your days with the Vietminh tonight?"

"You have already heard the stories a hundred times." Quan knew that to resist was futile, but Truong always had willing ears.

"Please Uncle, just once more?"

"Very well, once more. But this is the last time." Quan knew it would not be the last time.

Huntington Park, California.

The California sun was a welcome sight after three days of unusual rain. Jeffrey beamed with anticipation as his father finished assembling his new three speed English racer. His birthday wish had come true, and now he was the proud owner of a beautiful red full-size bike.

Pushing it out of the garage, Jeff followed his dad down the driveway to the sidewalk.

"Okay, son. I'll hold it steady while you get on." Patrick Riley held the handle bars while young Jeff mounted the bicycle with more than a little apprehension.

"Pedal the bike while I run along beside," said his father. "When you're ready, let me know and I'll let you go."

The duo took off down the sidewalk, Jeff pedaling furiously with his feet barely reaching the pedals. It quickly became obvious that the seat would have to be adjusted.

After passing three houses, Jeff worked up his nerve and signaled for this father to release his hold. It was just as well as Mr. Riley had done very little running since his discharge from the Marines after World War Two, and the short sprint was beginning to wind him. "Okay son, happy birthday." Jeff did well at first, but after crossing Mr. Huff's driveway, the bicycle began to waver. It edged to the strip of grass dividing the sidewalk from the street and then abruptly crossed it and went off the curb. The handle bars turned sideways and the bike fell over, tossing the eight-year-old onto the hard asphalt of the street.

Choking back tears, Jeff picked himself up and quickly examined the bicycle. Except for a scrape on one of the hand grips, it was unharmed.

"Alright son, get back on." Mr. Riley picked the bike up and stood ready for Jeff to mount.

"Not now, Dad. Maybe tomorrow."

"Now, son. You'll never learn unless you get right back on. You've just been given one of life's most basic lessons. Consider it a gift and remember it."

"But Dad..." Jeff hedged.

"NOW!"

Jeff reluctantly remounted the bike. Again he tried to retain control of the obstinate machine, but once more he found that there was more to it than he had anticipated.

When his father decided that Jeff had had enough for one day, he made Jeff push the bicycle back into the garage.

"Son, as you go through life, I want you to remember what happened today. There are many things that will hurt you, but you will learn something after each one."

That night, after dinner, Jeff sat on his bed in the solitude of his room and reflected on the days events. On his bedstand lay his 'coon skin cap that his dad had given him after the popularity of the television story swept the country. He picked up the cap and brushed the fur fondly. Davy Crockett wasn't a quitter, and Jeff, as many young American boys did, idolized Davy Crockett. Jeff would not be a quitter either.

Just then, his father came into the room and sat down on the bed next to him. "Ready for a bedtime story?"

Jeffrey beamed. "Yes sir.   How about 'Rikki-Tikki-Tavi'?"

Mr. Riley reached up to the shelf above his head and pulled down a well-worn black book. His father had read many of these stories from this book to him when he was Jeff's age.

"Well son, you sure do like Kipling. This must be the tenth time you've heard this story. Let's see here," Mr. Riley thumbed through the pages-- and began:

"This is the story of the great war that Rikki-Tikki-Tavi fought single-handed..."

Chapter One

Near Da Nang, Republic of Vietnam, September 1967

It wasn't a hard rain. But it was steady, and what there was of it was miserable enough. Large droplets of cold water slapped on the broad emerald leaves of the plants overhead, then streaked to the tips where they gathered to cascade off in small crystalline streams to the ground below. There, small puddles formed only to overflow into a network of rivulets that spread into larger pools. To the weary Marine, who lay in the mud in faded wet jungle utilities that almost gagged him with the mixed stench of mildew and day-old sweat, the rain was an enemy. He silently cursed the monsoon that turned his lair into a mud bath. The old hands had said that this was only the beginning. The rainy season wouldn't slacken until January. And it would get worse as black rain-swollen clouds rolled in off the South China Sea. Torrents of water would pelt the landscape, swelling the rivers and streams and flooding the rice paddies until movement in the lowlands around Da Nang became almost impossible. And the rain wasn't the only enemy. Of course there were the VC and NVA, with their booby traps and ambushes, but there were also poisonous snakes, diseases, jungle rot, back-breaking terrain, the insufferable heat--and insects. He hated the insects worst of all. They were the kings of infiltration. Creeping legions of them wearing their tiny armor, or squadrons with buzzing wings were everywhere. Fire ants, leeches, spiders, mosquitoes...

Another one! It felt like the bastard was drilling for oil on his neck. He wanted to slap it ever-so-badly, but he knew better. He reached up slowly, silently cursing the ineffectiveness of military-issue insect repellant, and rubbed it into oblivion, grinding its tiny body into the waxy green camouflage paint on his skin. He had learned a lot in his eight months in Vietnam, and one thing that a grunt in the field learned very quickly was that you didn't slap mosquitoes or other biting insects while sitting in an ambush position. Noise in the jungle could be hazardous to one's health. Any noise.

Ten hours before, under cover of early morning darkness, the squad had crept silently into the stand of thorny bamboo and broad-leafed banana trees. The ambushers had lain in the mud under the bushes all day, suffering first the heat, then the rain, and always the boredom as they waited for victims to find their way into the kill zone. As they waited, every other man tried to get some sleep. Fifty percent security was better than no rest at all.

Jeffrey Charles Riley, Corporal, USMC, the skinny nineteen-year-old blond-haired surfer kid from California, examined the palm of his hand. A tiny smear of blood mixed with green camouflage paint was all that remained of the voracious insect. He wiped it on his shirt front and re-grasped his M-14, then smirked with the realization that his shirt was as dirty as his body. And to think that he was the leader.

He hadn't wanted the "promotion," but his predecessor, Sergeant Cashio, had been killed two weeks before during a routine village sweep, victim of a spider-trap sniper. Now, as the only corporal-- and a boot corporal at that--the squad was his by fact of attrition--not desire.

Riley noted movement on the edge of his vision. He took his eyes off the trail and looked down. A six-inch long, slimy green leech slithered along the edge of a small puddle beside his left elbow as an occasional rain drop splattered near it. His first inclination was to chop it up with his K-bar, but he was too tired to put forth the effort.

The clouds grew darker and the rain began to intensify. It ran down his neck and off the edge of his green cotton utility cover into his eye, carrying a mixture of stinging, salty sweat with it. Riley blinked rapidly but it did little good. He slowly moved his head over to his shoulder to wipe it clear but succeeded in only smearing a swatch of camouflage paint off of his face.

Riley looked at his watch. The crystal was smeared with mud. He made a few swipes across his shirt front until he could read the dial. In less than an hour it would be dark. Good, he thought. At least the setting sun would reduce the possibility of detection and cool off the steaming jungle. He caught himself wishing for a slight breeze. That would help cover any inadvertent noises that the squad might make, and at the same time stir the damp stink of rotting vegetation that permeated everything from their nostrils to the pores of their skin.

Ten meters to Riley's right lay Private First Class Galleon. Toby Galleon had been Riley's friend since boot camp when individuals found that it was only possible to make it through recruit training after they learned to team up. Galleon, a dark-complected Spanish-Indian from Colorado and former Golden Gloves boxer, made a good friend and a reliable team mate. He also was next in line to take the team leader slot of the first fire team when Lance Corporal Edmonds--who was getting short--rotated home.

As it grew dusk, Galleon concentrated on the kill zone. If there was a good moon and the clouds weren't too thick, he would be able to see shadows, movement, something. But if there wasn't, and it was another pitch-black night, he would have to depend on his ears and his nose. He peered through the vertical stalks of the banana trees and green segmented tubes of huge Vietnamese bamboo to the trail to his front. He diverted his eyes momentarily, giving them a rest. He knew not to stare, but to glance around a given area to keep from seeing things that weren't there. Let 'em come tonight, he thought. "I just want to even up the score for Cashio," he whispered to himself. Too many times the squad had lain in ambush for endless hours, trapping only boredom and fatigue.

Galleon's thoughts drifted back to "Operation Bayonet". It had seemed like a routine sweep, and Cashio was no boot to combat, but something went wrong. They should have sensed it, but didn't until it was too late. Galleon was walking point, Riley following ten meters behind. They had both passed the same spot in the trail and were scouting up ahead when Cashio arrived there. He stopped at the edge of the trail to answer the PRC 6 walkie-talkie when it happened. One shot. Cashio pitched forward, jerked once and died.

The squad took up immediate security as Riley ran back to the stricken squad leader while yelling for the corpsman. There was no sign of a sniper, but they knew he was near.

"Lamb....you and Foster try to find that gook. He's real close. Hey Karlov, di-di back down the trail and find Doc. Tell 'em Cashio's been hit, and to hai-ako his ass up here mo-skoshe'. I think he's had it, but we need Doc to take over on that. Now move!" yelled Riley as he dragged Cashio's body into the brush next to the trail.

Private Eugene Lamb, the dark curly haired squad wiseacre, who had just made private for the third time after one of his traditional bouts with the bar girls and MPs in Da Nang, crept into the tree line behind the squad, his wiry body disappearing between tall thick stalks of bamboo. As he made his way around the edge of the small clearing, he examined every mound and depression for signs of a spider trap.

Foster, Lamb's short and stocky black partner who formed the other half of the salt-and-pepper team, followed. Within seconds he froze, signaled Lamb with a thumbs down, and pointed toward the ground about five meters to his front. Lamb eased over and pulled a grenade from his belt. Foster slowly stepped back and found a safe depression to lay behind as Lamb pulled the pin from the grenade.

Galleon watched all of this from his position of cover. He eased the safety off his M-14 and drew a bead near the spot that Lamb was approaching. Lamb laid the grenade on top of the spider trap's camouflaged lid, released the spoon, then retreated quickly to Foster's spot and ducked down. The grenade went off with a KA-WHUMP, raising dirt and leaves into the air in a brown dusty cloud that drifted over the watching squad. Just then the corpsman arrived, sliding into the brush next to Riley.

Foster and Lamb dragged the bloody, limp body of the sniper from the hole.

Galleon remembered the sniper that ended the life of Sergeant James A. Cashio. He was maybe fifteen years old at the most, and appeared to be a typical village peasant kid that had received the minimum amount of training and given a rusty old French rifle and a simple order: kill.

Toby felt guilt. He blamed himself for Cashio's death. After all, he was point on the sweep, and it was up to him to detect the enemy before he threatened the squad. In actuality, Cashio knew better than to stop in the open, and he knew better than to be seen talking on a radio in broad daylight with a tell-tale antenna sticking up, identifying him as a leader. But like everyone else who spent too many sleepless days and nights, he was tired. For one fleeting moment he also was careless. Now he was dead.

The black WD-1 commo wire tied to Galleon's wrist jerked once, then twice, bringing him back to the present. His heart jumped. Someone or something was approaching. He passed the signal down the line to Riley.

Riley immediately passed it along and shifted his prone body slightly to bring his rifle to bear on the trail. Most squad leaders carried a .45 automatic pistol, but Riley did not yet feel comfortable with anything but the rifle that had brought him this far. He eased the safety off.

To Riley's left, Eddie Karlov, the lanky "Mad Russian" with the Ichabod Crane ears and eagle-beak nose, slid the safety off his M-79 grenade launcher and rested it on a stake he had preset by cutting its height for elevation. He had previously picked a spot beyond the kill zone that seemed the most logical place gooks may try to escape to or seek refuge and cut the stake accordingly. He checked his safety--off. Satisfied, he waited.

Each squad member acted accordingly. It was automatic by now. The platoon had landed eight months before, and except for two replacements, all of them had been there that long. They had learned the hard way. And it had cost them. From the original forty-eight, the platoon was now down to thirty-four men including the lieutenant, the platoon sergeant, the right guide, and the corpsman. There might be fewer of them now, but they were smarter than they were then. They were also much more efficient.

As they watched, a water buffalo with a Vietnamese boy on its back walked down the trail. Riley relaxed and jerked the wire once. False alarm.

Just after midnight, shots broke the stillness to the east. Sporadic at first, then intensifying in crescendo until it became a small firefight. Someone was in contact. They could differentiate the distinctive sounds of the American weapons from the crack of the AK-47's and the SKS carbines. Soon 81 millimeter mortar and 105 millimeter howitzer parachute illumination rounds lit up the night sky, popping, then hissing in the distance near where the shots came from. Within a few minutes the shooting tapered off and the flares, followed by wispy trails of white smoke, drifted to the ground and burned out. Then it was silent again.

Riley shifted his body to work out the kinks. His sixth sense told him that something was going to happen and he wanted to be ready. He jerked the wire three times, then another three. It was the signal for one-hundred percent alert. He wanted everyone up.

At the end of the ambush line, near a bend in the trail and forming the base of the L formation, waited the patrol's M-60 machine gun manned by Lance Corporal Jack "Hillbilly" Thomas and his "A" gunner, PFC Darrell Simmons. Simmons eased himself up onto his elbows and once more checked the loaded belt of 7.62 millimeter ball ammo, every fifth round a tracer. Thomas made sure the cocking handle was locked into the forward position for the hundredth time and wished he could stand up for just a little while. His elbows were sore and raw from staying propped up under the gun for so long. At least the ground was soft and muddy this night. It would be much worse if it were clay-hard as it normally was.

Thomas liked his job. Here in Vietnam, he was important. He was needed. It was different here, not like Knoxville where he was just another kid on the block with nothing unusual about him to make him stand out. Here, his squad depended on him. He carried the major portion of the squad's firepower in his machine gun. He caressed it fondly in the dark. Twenty-six pounds of cool gray metal that was his life support at this end, and the enemy's death at the other. He felt a love for the gun that one might feel toward a well-trained attack dog that was loyal and obedient, so long as you held onto the leash and gave the commands. His dog could, as he was fond of reminding everyone, "bark here, but bite way over yonder." He checked the safety once more, wiped some water droplets off the rear sight aperture and settled back to wait.

For Thomas, waiting was the worst part of war. Some claimed it was death, while others maintained it was the climate, or exhaustion, or filth, or disease, or bad chow, or maybe something as simple as no mail. Thomas knew better. It was the waiting. In a combat zone, the eternal waiting for something to happen brought both boredom and apprehension. Boredom would make one lax, a dangerous situation in itself, and apprehension could open the door to fear and the realization that there was no such thing as immortality. Anyone could get in the way of a bullet.

They came just before 0300 hours in the morning. Five of them. Murphy detected them first. He was stationed on the far right flank as security and it was his job to spot anyone coming into the ambush from that side. He signaled with one, then two rapid tugs on the wire, Then he froze. They were to pass him and continue on into the kill zone. After they passed, he melted further back into the brush. He noted that they were indeed carrying weapons, a prerequisite to opening fire, and one of them was limping. They were probably the ones who were in the fire fight earlier to the east.

Murphy counted to ten and held his breath. It wouldn't be long now. Any second Riley would initiate the ambush with a grenade, signaling Thomas to open up with a long burst from his machine gun by firing down the long axis of the trail. He also knew that he was near the receiving end of the cone of fire from the M-60 when it did open up, and took cover accordingly.

At that instant, the night was lit with a blinding flash of an M-26 fragmentation grenade, followed immediately by a string of red tracers arcing down the trail.

Riley looked up after the grenade went off just in time to see Thomas's burst of fire slice through the smoke into the two lead Vietnamese, spinning them to the ground. Their three companions tried to turn back and run the other way in panic, but were cut down by Karlov who sailed a 40 millimeter grenade from his M-79 in front of them with a muffled "PUNK", followed by the white flash of the explosion.

"Tail-end charlie" was thrown backwards, dropping his AK and rolling on the ground. The two remaining Viet Cong came under fire from Galleon and the rest of the squad on his end. They too went down.

Two more M-79 grenades and a trip flare sailed into the kill zone. Riley wished they had claymore mines. He would have liked to use them to initiate the ambush, but couldn't get any in time for this patrol. The trip flare illuminated the area with a pop and a smoking sizzle just as the M-79 rounds exploded in a final act of destruction.

"Search team out!" commanded Riley as he stood up and changed magazines in his rifle. Galleon and Lamb stepped out into the trail as Foster covered them.

Lamb picked up the weapons while Galleon searched the bodies after putting a bullet through each head before moving or rolling the corpses over. When he had stripped them of documents, notebooks, ammo pouches and any other usable piece of intelligence, he signaled Riley and the others and moved back off the trail.

It was time to get the hell out of there and Riley knew it. They were deep in indian country and soon all the indians in the world would be coming down upon them. He'd been there before. First it would be the sound of the drums. Great hollow logs beat in a rapidly building tatoo, picked up by other drums in the distance that would telegraph their presence to every gook with a rifle in the area. When the drums started he always felt like Custer must have when the 7th Cavalry was forced to dismount on that hillside in South Dakota a hundred years before--or Davy Crockett at the Alamo when Santa Ana ordered his bugler to play the Deguello. He unwound the commo wire from his wrist and let it fall to the ground.

"Let's go," he yelled. No point in being quiet now. The whole world knew they were there. There was a time to be the mongoose, and a time to gracefully get the hell out of Dodge.

And this was it.

Chapter Two

Lieutenant Harvey "Smudge" Smith briefly scanned the instruments and turned his attention to the cockpit's side window and the landscape rolling by below. As usual it was beautiful--at least from this altitude. Except for the occasional shell crater or column of smoke rising from distant operations, there was little evidence of war from his lofty perch. Shoeless kids wearing cone-shaped straw hats sat on the backs of dark gray water buffalos grazing contentedly in the fields; lines of old men and women stood bent at the waist, knee-deep in rice paddy water, as they cut the last of the season's crop before the paddies became flooded with the rains; brown rivers and streams separated the checkerboard of rice and sugar cane fields as they meandered, almost overflowing their banks, toward the sea; every shade of green presented itself to the observer so inclined to notice, and it all melded to form a picture that would fit perfectly in National Geographic magazine. For the moment, there was no war.

Smith yawned. This flight, other than having to dodge the intermittent misty gray columns of monsoon rain, should be another milk run. He thought of the different missions he and his crew had flown in the past six months and this one, in comparison, should pose no problem at all. It was a pussy run. And on a day like this, it would be a flight to enjoy.

Next to Smith sat his co-pilot, Lieutenant Yoshiro Tanaka. Tanaka was a black-haired twenty-four year-old Nisei from Los Angeles who took war as seriously as his samurai forbearers. Tanaka also scanned the countryside, but not because he was impressed by its beauty. He studied the terrain looking for landmarks. Each glance brought his gaze back to the map clipped to his kneeboard where his gloved hand occasionally drew an "x" and noted the time. He was a perfectionist who insisted on accuracy in everything he did and would not allow his attention to be diverted long enough to play tourist--or get them lost.

The thundering green Sikorsky, its 1,525 horsepower Wright Cyclone piston engine maintaining a throaty roar, lulled Smith further into a sense of security with its even rhythm. Above, almost hypnotic in their motion, the four main rotor blades cast stacatto shadows over the cockpit as the helicopter drove on.

And there were no troops to worry about. In the troop compartment below and behind the cockpit, the cavernous fuselage contained only stacks of orange and blue mail bags, manila colored wax-surfaced boxes of C-rations, a lashed-down row of green five-gallon water cans and a few wooden cases of small arms ammunition. On his seat at the edge of the single door, gripping his M-60 machine gun, sat the third member of the crew-- and only enlisted man--who performed the dual functions of crew chief and door gunner.

Corporal Stevens, known simply as "chief" to Smith and Tanaka, liked the supply runs. All they had to do was come to a hover over a dry piece of real estate previously secured by the grunts and kick out the sacks and boxes marked for that location. It beat the hell out of delivering troops into a hot landing zone on a heli-team mission. Though they might draw a few stray rounds, it would be nothing like what they could expect to encounter if they were dumping grunts into an LZ ringed by VC armed with heavy machine guns and RPGs. He shifted his posture in the narrow nylon seat and tried to relax.

They had all been up since 0400 and everyone on board was tired. Each morning it was the same thing: A mission briefing, which grew briefer each day they were in Vietnam as the crews found themselves flying repeatedly into the same areas with the same cargos. Then the pre-flight inspection of the aircraft while the support troops loaded it, followed by the start-up, with blue smoke billowing out beneath the cowling as the big piston engine caught, fired, and finally settled into a mellow roar. The rotor blades by then had begun to turn, slowly at first then building in rpm as the clutch brought them up to speed. A few minutes of warm-up, a magneto and manifold pressure check, then a roll-out to take-off position. It was all quite simple, and always the same. To Smith, they were a mosaic of sounds and smells that began with reveille. First the smell and bitter taste of mess tent coffee in the dark of the early morning, then the sound of pots and pans being banged about in the still, damp air. Then breakfast done, the sound of the waves crashing on the nearby beach as he walked toward the flight line, the coughs and roars of engines starting on the ramp, and finally the tang of the burning oil when his engine caught--it all melded together in a kaleidoscope of familiar sights, sounds and smells.

But the daily routine would cease when the crimson sun rose over the turquoise waters of the

South China Sea. It was then, when the swarms of H-34s rose to fly into another day, that the daily routine was quickly replaced with the fear of the unknown. The question of what the next few hours would hold and who would return to fly another day--and who might not--entered the minds of each and every crewman as the machines banked away for their assigned destinations.

Tanaka studied the terrain passing by below, quickly checked his map and keyed the intercom. "Should be getting close now."

"Yeah, okay...this should be the last drop, then we can head home," answered Smudge. "Home" was their base, the Marine Air Facility airfield north of Marble Mountain on China Beach, a mass of green canvas tents, sand bag bunkers, steel perspex mat landing ramps, and concertina wire fences. Not exactly barracks-room comfort, but far better than a foxhole in the field.

"Good. I still have a hangover from last night," said Tanaka reminding Smith about the poker game and his bout with Tiger Piss beer. "I could use some down time."

"And I could use some R and R," grinned Smith. "Maybe a few days in Bangkok, or better yet, Australia."

"Yeah, that'd be great. But I'd settle for just twenty-four hours of rack time. Undisturbed. Know what I mean?"

Before the Smudger could answer, their conversation was broken by the voice of Stevens over the intercom from his isolated perch at the open door of the troop compartment. "We gettin' close yet, sir?"

Tanaka thought about him sitting back there alone in the troop compartment. When they were on cargo hauls, Stevens had no troops to keep him company and the pilots, sitting "upstairs" in the cockpit, were only visible to him in the form of two pairs of lower legs and combat boots. He remembered a crew chief once telling him of losing a pilot he was particularly close to. They were taking ground fire, Chinese .51s, when the aircraft lurched and pitched suddenly to one side. When he looked up expecting to see the pilot's boots busy on the pedals, he found them instead tucked back under the seat bottom, motionless. As the co-pilot took over and regained control of the ship a bright stream of blood dripped from the pilot's seat to the bulkhead below, then down into the troop compartment. The chief knew the pilot was hit-- probably dead--and there was nothing he could do for him. And if the co-pilot lost it, there was nothing he could do for any of them except ride it in. He was isolated, and very alone. At least Tanaka had a set of controls that gave him a handle on his fate.

"About five minutes, Danny," answered Yoshi.

"Thanks, Mister Tanaka." It was evident to Tanaka that the young crew chief was nervous. He always was when they began an approach to an LZ. He would be a prime target for enemy gunners who would concentrate on first knocking out the single machine gun, then worrying about the aircraft. This

Stevens knew by experience. But even if he was under fire he would do his job. He always did.

As they neared the designated location, they could see a puff of purple smoke beginning to drift in the wind at about ten o-clock, a thousand feet below.

"There it is," said Smudge, nodding his head toward the rising column.

"Right, I'll call grape." Tanaka keyed his mike button for the radio transmission to the line company waiting for their precious re-supply and identified the color. The line company commander, Charlie-Six Actual, confirmed. This ritual told the chopper pilots that it wasn't a Vietcong ruse to sucker them into a trap.

Smudger circled once and, after watching the smoke drift to determine wind direction, descended to a high hover. At fifty feet over the peninsula of land that jutted out into the rice paddies from the village encircled by the Marine company, Smith told Stevens to "GO!"

Danny began throwing out the mail bags as quickly as possible since he knew that the mail was more important to the waiting grunts than anything else. And if they took fire and had to leave, at least the grunts had their letters from home. Good ol' Suzy Snatchtail, the best morale builder since Chesty Puller. Give the grunts a reason to fight, or at least a reason to live, and the war was as good as won.

He was careful to hit the dry land this time. He had long ago learned that the grunts took a dim view of wet mail and runny ink after retrieving mail bags from the rice paddies. And there was no worse ground fire in the world than that of a pissed-off Marine line company.

They were lucky this time. They managed the re-supply mission without mishap and soon Smudge banked the helicopter away from the edge of the ville, nosed it over and pulled up on the collective stick to increase both airspeed and lift. It was time to head home--mission completed.

Stevens breathed a sigh of relief as he watched the rain- swollen rice paddies sink slowly away. It was beginning to rain again and mist began to gather and hang in the air. But it wouldn't be long before he could relax in his semi-dry tent, re-read his mail from his girl, open a lukewarm Bai Muoi Bai beer, and maybe--if Charlie didn't play mortar tag--get a decent night's sleep. He felt good. He'd made it through another day.

So far.

Chapter Three

It was shortly after the sun rose over the coastal mountains at the Hai Van pass, that Peterson detected movement behind them.

They had successfully pulled out of the ambush location and made their way across the stinking waist deep paddies to a dry Vietnamese cemetery about a klick away when Peterson saw them. Actually he sensed them more than saw them. He had pulled Tail-end Charlie on most of their patrols. He liked the job, and he was good at it. He liked to brag that he personally "covered all their asses".

Using hand and arm signals, he had the patrol halt and take up security positions while he scanned the three-foot high rice stalks behind them. There it was again. A movement. Just a fleeting movement...then another. That was the guerrillas way. Slow, careful and yet an occasional flash or dash from one point or another. The Viet Cong were stalking them now. It was obvious that they did not have enough force to attack, or they would have. Charlie would not mess with the Marines until he grossly outnumbered them. Then the fight would be quick--just long enough to either inflict as much damage as possible before fading back into the terrain, or to annihilate the enemy. Riley made his way back to Peterson and enquired with his eyes.

"Gooks...three...maybe four of 'em. Hundred meters," whispered Peterson nodding in the direction of the last movement.

"Right. We'll kick up the pace a bit and see what happens. We ain't got enough ammo left for a big show. Keep your eyes on 'em," ordered Riley getting up and moving back up the column in a crouch low enough to keep below the rice stalks. The Marines knew how to play this game as well.

Nguyen Van Truong, the Viet Cong ha-si, or corporal, who first detected the capitalist murderers trail after the fighting last night, edged his way out of the paddy water to a prone position on the muddy dike. Yes, there is sign. The distinct impressions of American jungle boots. Between eight and ten Yankees had passed this way within the last hour. Truong was very proud of his tracking ability. It is what had gotten him promoted. Van Truong had little formal education, but had spent most of his early years hunting animals for food near his village of Ho Nam Khe on the Laotian border of North Vietnam. After his uncle's tutoring, he became the best tracker in the village.

He signaled his two companions, Tran and Hai, to close in on him. "Go back and tell the trung-'uy we have found the Americans, and say they are heading toward Khuong My. We will follow. Now hurry!" he ordered Tran. "Now we will see what they do," he whispered as he raised his eyes above the shoots of rice.

Just before they got to the rally point marked on their maps north of Chili Ridge, it began. Drums. When the Viet Cong in this area wanted to alert others of enemy presence or call a get-together, they beat on huge hollow tree trunks that rumbled a haunting tattoo that carried for thousands of meters. The beat would start slow and rhythmically increase in tempo to a rapid roll, then stop only to start all over again. This would be heard and repeated from other locations and the "word" would spread.

Riley counted the drums. Four...no five. Two behind, one distantly to the right and two ahead. That changed their plans. They had to divert their route back to the perimeter toward the side where no drums sounded.

Galleon could almost read Riley's mind and with only a glance over his shoulder, confirmed the new direction. The patrol moved off the dike and started out into the paddies on a short cut that would hopefully throw their followers off. It was a long shot, but it worked for a little while.

When the Marines had reached the other side of the paddy, it was obvious that the VC would marshal their guerrillas faster than Riley had anticipated. They weren't going to make it back to the perimeter, and they were still too far out for a ground reactionary force to be of timely assistance.

Riley made his way up to Galleon as he grabbed the PRC-6 that hung suspended by its single strap around his neck. "Toby, head about zero-eight-five. We should come to a rise in the ground and have a dry spot to defend and use as an LZ."

"About how far?" Galleon asked.

"'Bout five hundred meters." Riley keyed the radio and began calling for a helicopter extraction.

Peterson could still tell the VC were there. He only wished he had something to leave them. A mine would be nice, but wishing and having were two different things. The favorite saying of Staff Sergeant Hays, the big black platoon sergeant from Alabama, echoed in his mind; "It's better to have it and not need it, than need it and not have it--"

"Trung-uy!" puffed Tran loudly as he slid into the tunnel, "We found the Yankees!"

"Oh?" said the lieutenant looking up from writing a message to the thieu-ta, Phong's major.

"Comrade Phong, they are only two kilometers distant. Ha-si Truong say they go to Khuong My," said the sixteen year old private.

"Very good. We will signal our comrades."

In the helicopter, Tanaka heard the radio call from MAG Sixteen Operations and recognized the familiar voice of Captain Beau "Stonewall" Jackson; "Iron Hawk two niner, this is Sultan one zero, over."

"This is Hawk two niner, over?" replied Yoshi into his boom mike.

"Two niner, do you have fuel for an extraction north of Chili Ridge? Over." came the voice mixed with static.

Tanaka and Smith eyed the fuel gauge and checked the map. If they grabbed a heading right now, they could make the pick-up and then the air base at Da Nang and refuel there.

"Roger, we got enough motion lotion for that and a straight run to the air base."

"Understand...ready to copy coordinates?"

"Roger," said Tanaka as he pulled a yellow lead pencil from his knee board.

"Eight eight five...six two niner...a single squad requesting evacuation. LZ may be hot, do you copy? Over?"

"Understand eight eight five, six two niner...squad...hot LZ," repeated Yoshi as he wrote.

"Affirmative, see you when you get home, one zero...out."

Tanaka looked over at Smudge and pointed the direction to the new heading while maintaining his best inscrutable oriental face. The Smudger always accused him of being "inscrutable," the result of watching too many Charlie Chan movies.

"Chief, we got a new mission," Smith informed Stevens over the intercom. "Stand by to pick up some grunts who may have some unfriendly company."

"Okay Skipper," answered the crew chief as he slid his helmet visor down over his eyes and checked his machine gun once more. "Shit. Here we go again."

Now that they were getting close to the point on the map that Riley figured would be a good place to await a chopper, Riley suddenly heard yelling around them in the distant tree lines. Then the shooting began. AK and SKS fire buzzed overhead and started to drop toward the Marines as the pursuers found the range.

"Hold your fire until we get set up and you have a definite target," yelled Riley just as Galleon and the rest of the squad crawled out of the paddy to the dry piece of ground that contained an overgrown cemetery and a one-room concrete Buddhist temple. The small island was surrounded by rice paddies on all sides, and was barely large enough to hold the deployed squad. The temple was little more than a shrine with a pillared front porch, a small window on each wall, and several ornate carvings on the roof crest.

"I got some at three o'clock" said Thomas as he elevated the rear sight on his machine gun for the correct range, locked the buttstock into his shoulder and flicked the safety to "fire."

"Rock an' roll whenever you're ready, but keep the bursts short. I got Battalion on the hook and a chopper's on the way, but it could be fifteen or twenty minutes," yelled Riley rolling behind a flat concrete tombstone.

"Okay gomers, it's Doctor Death, the Master of Disaster and his faithful sidekick the All Night Mover. We are the heart breakers and the life takers...." yelled Thomas as he took up the slack on the trigger to send a burst of 7.62 millimeter arcing out to the little men in black darting between the clumps of bamboo. The tracers marked their path in bright burning spots of red with a few ricocheting off rocks, flying skyward.

The returning AK and SKS fire was supplemented by the stacatto bursts of a PKS machine gun. Thomas would have some competition now. Riley hoped they wouldn't take any mortar fire.

Just then, a solitary little man in black popped up above the tall rice stalks not more than seventy-five meters in front of them and shouldered an RPG-7. A puff of smoke erupted behind the tube and a B-40 rocket flew straight at the small perimeter of Marines. It swooshed by and impacted against the temple, blowing a jagged hole in the concrete wall, filling the air around it with cement dust.

For his sin, he was blown backwards in small puffs of black silk and pink mist. The Viet Cong had the unfortunate luck to have stood up in front of Murphy and his fully automatic Mk II M-14.

The fire fight continued, with the VC maneuvering constantly for more advantageous positions.

"Riley! They're behind us!" yelled Karlov, loading an HE round into his '79.

"Take Skater and Peewee with you and lob some shit out there. Try to try to keep 'em pinned down until we can get pulled out," ordered Riley as he jammed another magazine into his rifle.

Karlov crawled quickly past two Marines who were busy firing over a log and said: "you two guys come with me, we gotta cover the rear from that temple there."

Within two minutes, the VC who had made their way around behind the Marines were introduced to the accuracy of Karlov's grenade launcher and the capabilities of the Marine riflemen. One of the Viet Cong died immediately in mid-stride. The crack of the '79 grenades with their bright flash and black smoke cloud easily held the VC advance from the rear. If ammo would only hold out....

"Where is that mortar?" asked Phong of his trung-si, Sergeant Quan.

"They should be ready soon, comrade. They had to bring it from where it was well buried," answered the old man who had fought with the Viet

Minh against the French at Dien Bien Phu so many
years before.   For Quan it was still the same war,
only the enemy's uniforms and flag had changed.

"They are ready now, comrade trung-uy,"
came the voice behind Phong from the boy who had
just ran up.

"Give the order to fire!" commanded Phong
with a grin.

Just as the first 82 millimeter mortar rounds
impacted near the Marine positions, a sound could
be heard that gladdened the hearts of the grunts and
hit the Viet Cong leader like a fist in the chest.

The beautiful sound of a big Pratt and
Whitney radial engine and the rhythmic beats of the
four big Sikorsky rotor blades began to fill the air;
distant at first, but rapidly building in crescendo as
the machined approached. Phong knew he would
have to act quickly.

In the cockpit, the Smudger and Tanaka had a birds-
eye view of the fight. The Marines were in a ragged
perimeter in a small cemetery that was surrounded
by acres of flooded rice paddies. Little men in
black could be seen struggling through the muddy
water as they attempted to maneuver for advantage
as blasts of dirt rose skyward from around and
within the Marine perimeter. The LZ was definitely
hot.

"Yoshi...try and get us some air support.
We need to knock out that tree line on the west.
That is probably where the mortar forward observer
is," ordered Smith.

"Okay Skipper," said Tanaka as he clicked the radio dial to the correct frequency. "Fire Cloud six six...this is Iron Hawk two-niner, mission request, over?"

Two tries later the voice came over the earphones, "Iron Hawk two-niner, this is Fire Cloud six six...send mission, over?"

"We're on an extraction with a hot LZ just north of Chili Ridge, what have ya got? over?"

"All we have in that vicinity is a mix-and-match team, state nature of target, over?"

"Victor Charlie complement in tree line, maybe a platoon reinforced with mortars, can you cover, over? asked Yoshi.

"Stand by, out," came the efficient but terse reply.

Twenty seconds later, Yoshi's helmet reverberated with a new voice. "Iron Hawk two-niner, you got Silver Lance four zero, the grunts salvation and the gooks castration. Do you copy, over?"

"That's affirmative Lance four-zero, are you carrying a full load?" asked Tanaka in reference to the four M-60 machine guns on the gun ship and the two pods of 2.75 inch HVAR rockets on the rocket ship.

"Aye aye cap'n Bligh, that you Tanaka?" asked the voice in its cocky southern drawl.

"That's affirmative "Reb", glad you guys could make it," grinned Tanaka as he thought of the stocky Huey gunship driver with the Confederate Flag painted on the nose of his UH-1.

"I hope this is a better tea party than the last one you guys threw."

"By the looks of this action, this ain't no tea party. Get your asses over here and cover us. We gotta get in there quick!" said Tanaka hurriedly. The VC were beginning to get organized for an assault, and wanted to do something before the helicopter could intervene.

"We're on our way, estimate one zero mike," came a more serious reply. Johnny "Reb" Johnson rolled the turbine powered Bell helicopter to the left, and his wing-man in the rocket chopper, Captain "Midnight" Lawson, followed suit. Fun and games, girls. More fun and games, he thought grimly.

"They must go NOW! We cannot wait longer," said Phong dropping his binoculars around his neck and standing up. "Tell Truong to attack!"

"Yes, comrade trung-uy," said the old sergeant obediently. Even the officers were the same. There is so much that this child does not know, thought Quan.

Truong saw the signal and ordered the attack for a squad that had been sent to reinforce him. They stood up on line and moved forward, trying to stay as low as possible until they could close with the imperialists.

Truong watched as one American moved from position to position, giving commands. He must be the leader, thought Truong, raising his rifle. Just as the Vietcong took aim, a mortar round burst near the Americans, causing one to stumble. The

Marine's helmet fell off, exposing a crop of light blond hair.

 Riley retreived his helmet and crawled behind another grave marker.

"RILEY! Only got a hundred rounds left!" yelled Thomas as he turned toward his assistant gunner. "Lamb! Still got that assault pack?"

"Yeah, here it comes," Lamb shouted back as he unstrapped the small green cloth container with the M-60 ammo belt, and threw it over to Simmons while Thomas changed barrels and dropped the smoking one on the ground.

"Why the hell don't that chopper get his ass down here and pick us up?" asked Lamb.

"Would you?" answered Galleon as he noticed a more concentrated movement to their front. He jammed his last magazine into his rifle, worked the bolt and brought the stock to his cheek. "Pass the word. Here they come!"

"Okay Hawk, we got the action...we're rollin' in and rollin' hot! Stay the fuck outta Dodge until we get through," advised Reb.

"Okay, you got it," keyed Tanaka.

The first Huey in was the rocket ship. Midnight Lawson lined up on the tree line that appeared to be the most likely spot for any large element of Victor Charlies and the FO for the enemy mortar. When they popped over the trees, the target area was in their sights and Lawson fired three pair. Flames sparked back from the rear of the launch tubes as the 2.75 inch rockets, their noses filled with high explosive, accelerated into the emerald green vegetation. As they exploded into fiery billows of flame and smoke, the Huey banked away sharply and began evasive maneuvers.

Phong had just entered the rice paddies when the helicopter came into view over the treeline. Surprised, he stopped immediately and stared at it. It was his worst fear. Caught in the open, there was no place to seek shelter from the onslaught that he knew would follow.

Then the beast breathed fire from its sides and the tree line behind him erupted into hell. Shards of shattered branches, stones and dirt flew through the air and showered down around him. Phong, spurred back into action by the concussions, dove forward into the protective embrace of the paddy water.

There was a splash next to him. He turned to see what large object had fallen so near, but was shocked at what greeted him.   It was Quan. The old sergeant, his friend from many battles, lay floating face down next to him. Phong rolled him over.

The old man was still alive. But Phong knew he would soon die. The wounds, even if not critical by modern standards, would prove fatal in Phong's area of operations. He had almost no medical support, and almost any trauma, after the onset of infection, would end in fever-wracked death.

As the helicopter banked away and climbed for altitude, Phong dragged Quan to a nearby dike.

"We will return for you later, old friend. But now I must rejoin the battle."

Quan tried to answer, but could not seem to muster enough air in his lungs to make a sound. Each breath was becoming increasingly painful, and his vision was beginning to dim. He had seen many men die and knew that his fate had been sealed. Even if he survived this day, it was only a matter of time. He could still hear the battle raging and knew that out there, somewhere, was Truong.

Truong stood and, waving his AK-47 assault rifle over his head to show its fixed spike bayonet, screamed "ATTACK...ATTACK!"

Chapter Four

Just as Reb pulled up at the end of his run, he banked right to admire his handy work. The treeline, which still sparkled with small fires scattered along its base, was quickly becoming shrouded in smoke.

"Looks good to me. Let's grab some sky and see if we can lay some heat someplace else while the '34 picks up those grunts."

"Roger that," answered his co-pilot, John Whitehorse. John "Chief" Whitehorse was a big

Osage indian from Oklahoma whose parents used the money they made from the oil leases on their property to give John the college education that eventually led to his present state of affairs as a Marine Corps officer. "I think I saw some gooks in the rice on the west side of the Marine positions."

"Let's check it out." Reb banked into a turn to take them back over the fight and keyed his intercom. "Keep an eye out to starboard, Bobby."

"Aye-aye sir," the door gunner replied. Corporal Bobby Jenkins braced himself against the pedestal mounted M-60 and studied the green landscape rolling by below. He knew only too well that a well placed round in his helicopter would make him an instant grunt, forced to join those below--if he survived the crash. Jenkins doubled as the crew chief, and he considered the machine to be his personal property. He only loaned it to the pilots for each mission. Whenever they landed, the pilots did a short post-flight inspection, then turned it back over to him. Except for the few hours each day spent in the air, it was in his custody. He took care of the aircraft like it was a part of the family. Not only the pilots, but his own life depended upon his meticulous attention to the machine.

"You still with me Midnight?" Reb's voice came over the radio.

"You betcha, son," Lawson responded. "We're on your six at fifty meters, wanna go again?"

"Roger. We're lookin' for targets of opportunity now. Chief thinks he saw some dinks back by the grunt firefight out in the paddy. I'll make a pass. If we take fire, follow me in and fire 'em up."

Reb located the dike where Chief had seen activity, and began his dive. As they plunged earthward, he could see a line of black uniformed figures moving toward the surrounded Marines. But it was apparent that the grunts had not spotted the VC because of the high rice stalks. Reb and Chief could also see the Sikorsky making its final approach to the clearing outside the temple. The crew chief was firing his machine gun from the door in an attempt to cover the grunts, who were desperately trying to disengage long enough to reach the helicopter. As the H-34 slowed and settled to a hover, red dust blasted away and swirled up in twisting clouds around the great blades that partially obscured the lumbering beast.

"Smudge and Tanaka are gettin' ready to take hits and don't know it. Do you see those gooks on line?" asked Reb over the radio to Midnight.

"Affirmative.   Here we go, rollin' hot," replied Lawson nosing his ship over for the attack. "Follow us in and we'll try to divert their fire."

Truong ducked as the first helicopter passed low overhead, and puzzled as to why it had not fired upon them. Then he saw the second machine bearing down. They were caught in the open, at the sharp end of an armed helicopter. They couldn't take cover and they couldn't run. There was only one thing they could do in such a predicament.

"Shoot at the aircraft!" screamed Truong. "Shoot at the aircraft!"

Billowing balls of fire and muddy water marked the impact of the rockets. Midnight pulled the Huey into a tight right bank to evade the ground fire, then quickly jinked left behind a stand of trees.

"How'd that look to you?" he asked his co-pilot, Lyman Jones.

"Right on, Cap'n. I don't think we took any hits, but they were sure tryin'."

Truong's men didn't have the correct lead when the helicopter with the rockets came over, but they did when the first machine approached the second time. Four of Truong's guerrillas had died in the initial attack. It was almost impossible to move quickly in the rice field. They could only duck behind dikes. More would have died had the mud not absorbed much of the Yankee rocket's blast.

Johnson lined the figures up in his sight as well as he could and tried to steady the ship for his shot, but the vertical bounce from a slightly out-of-track main rotor blade forced him to simply spray the general area and hope for the best. Damn it! he said to himself through clenched teeth. He had told the maintenance officer about the track problem last week. It should have been fixed.

Just as the green tadpole-shaped aircraft finished its run, several AK rounds"thunked" into the ship. The first penetrated the main transmission casing, destroying a critical bearing. The second entered the compressor section of the engine, broke two rapidly spinning compressor blades, throwing the wheel out of balance and setting up a screaming high frequency vibration that was immediately felt in the cockpit. The broken blades exited the case and cut a fuel line, allowing a thin stream of high pressure JP-4 to spray into the hot engine compartment. The third severed a flight control hydraulic servo line.

"Main transmission chip light," announced the big indian as the yellow light blinked on the Christmas Tree warning light panel.

"Shit! We've lost hydraulics. Help me with the controls!" yelled Reb.

The vibration from the disabled engine immediately intensified as the engine began to ingest itself. The Low RPM Warning Horn blared as the engine decelerated through 6200 rpm.

"Shutting down!" yelled Reb, closing the throttle grip and attempting to enter auto-rotation. "Brace yourselves!"

Whitehorse squeezed the radio transmit button and broadcast on "guard," the frequency that all aircraft and installations monitored for aircraft in trouble. "Lance Four Zero...we're hit. Going down southwest of Iron Hawk's LZ." He couldn't spout off the coordinates from memory but knew MAG-16 would know from the mission board by checking Smith's and Tanaka's mission.

Wisps of black smoke began to seep into the cockpit, indicating a possible engine fire. Ahead, a line of ninety-foot tall bamboo and hardwood trees approached at eighty knots. If they went in short of the trees, the gooks would have them dead to rights.

If they managed to clear them and make it to the paddies on the opposite side, they could buy some breathing space before they could be picked up.

"We gonna make it over those trees?" asked Reb.

"All we can do is try."

Both pilots fought the stiff controls, trying desperately to override the failed hydraulic system. Reb glanced at the panel. The Rotor rpm needle was quickly dropping, indicating a bleed-off of rotor rpm--and with it, lift. It if drooped too far, the machine would simply fall to earth out of control. He lowered the collective in a desperate attempt to recapture some rpm. He rode it carefully. Lowered too much and they would plummet to earth like a stone, not enough and they would lose all lift and crash. In any event, they would lose altitude, and possibly not make it to the trees. But it would do little good to clear the trees only to roll up in a ball of flaming aluminum on the other side.

"Come on baby, you can do it, you can do it!" coaxed Reb. Then, keying the intercom, "We're gonna make it...we're gonna make it! At that moment, the crippled smoking helicopter crossed the tree line--and would have made it had it not been for the toes of the skids striking a branch, causing the machine to nose over. Reb pulled back on the cyclic with both hands. Little control remained, but every muscle in his arms strained as he fought to flair the machine. If he couldn't raise the nose to slow their forward speed, they would impact the paddies like a two-ton brick. At first, the machine began to respond. But only enough altitude remained to allow it to pitch up to a slightly nose high attitude before impacting with a glancing blow on the paddy's surface. The spinning rotor blades flexed down and struck the tail boom, severing it. The force threw the vertical stabilizer and tail rotor over a hundred meters away from the main fuselage, imbedding it into the soft mud of a dike. With the loss of directional control, the machine spun ninety degrees to the left and tried to roll up on its right side. The main rotor blades dug into the mud and water of the paddy and, slinging debris and vegetation skyward, lurched to a stop. This action forced what remained of the fuselage back to a semi-level position. For five full seconds no one inside moved. Then smoke began to fill the cabin.

"Switches off..." began Chief.

"Fuck the switches!" shouted Reb as he clawed at his harness buckles. "Get the hell out of here! This thing is gonna blow!"

Chief threw his door open and waded into the thigh-deep muddy water. He stopped after only a few struggling steps and glanced back to the rear compartment. Bobby, looking quite pissed as the surveyed the smoking hulk, was busy dismounting his gun. Reb was out on the other side making his way toward higher ground. A few minutes before they had been predators in the sky, masters of mens' fates, kings of the clouds, possessors of over a million dollars worth of taxpayers equipment, and now they were now reduced to a tiny island of humble humanity cast adrift in the middle of a war zone by a few tiny bullets fired by half-educated peasants who happened to get lucky. Hell was erupting around them and soon the hunters would become the hunted. All that expensive equipment, only seconds ago a deadly weapons system, now lay like so much junk in some farmer's field.

The Huey didn't explode. Curling black smoke began to rise from the engine compartment, then flames could be seen licking from around the cowling. Chief joined Reb in a small stand of high grass on a piece of dry ground, and Bobby, the M-60 and ammo belt weighing him down, straggled up within minutes. As they watched, what was left of their green steed quickly began to burn with increasing intensity. The final insult came when Reb saw the flames reach the nose and began to curl up around the Confederate flag painted there.

The flag seemed to linger for a moment. Then, as the heat intensified, the bottom colors of the Stars and Bars began to blacken. The plexiglass windshield above, then the broken chin bubbles below, turned gray and began to sag as they melted. Then the aluminum skin itself started to glow red as hot spots appeared. The flag was last. Like a color photo on a newspaper held over a match, the emblem glowed briefly...then disappeared.

"Looks like they made it out. I'll make one pass to check the area, then we'll drop in and grab 'em," said Lawson, eyeballing the burning wreckage and the three tiny figures in flight suits waving their arms.

"It's a long walk home, and the neighborhood is not very friendly."

Chapter Five

Stevens swung the jumping M-60 to the left and fired a long burst at a clump of bushes. He had seen movement there on their approach and gave it a good hosing. No one came out or returned fire. He glanced up from the sights and saw the grunts beginning to gather for extraction.

As the big helicopter settled its weight onto the oleo strut landing gear, bouncing slightly as it tested the ground, Riley signaled the squad to withdraw to the gaping door. Purple smoke drifted across the clearing and was soon joined by white HC smoke to add some concealment to the withdrawing Marines.

"Get 'em in here! We gotta get the hell out of here MO SKOSHE'!" Stevens yelled to Riley, who had just positioned himself next to the door to count his men as they scrambled into the helicopter.

"Hang on! I got two behind the pagoda. They'll be here in a sec!" Riley yelled back over the engine noise, looking for Peewee and the Slacker.

Two concussions from grenades were felt in rapid succession just as Peewee and Slacker rounded the corner. They sprinted toward the helicopter, pausing every few steps to fire a few shots behind them. The VC were closing in from the rear.

Thomas threw his machine gun on the deck of the helicopter and climbed up on the tire to get to the door when Simmons screamed out in pain behind him.

"Darryl!" shouted Thomas, jumping down to help his assistant gunner.

"Gimme a hand...we'll get him up!" ordered Riley, grabbing the wounded Marine by his canvas belt suspenders. Blood could be seen through one of Simmons calves. Riley and Thomas slung him into the troop compartment and crawled in after Peewee and Slacker brought up the rear.

Smudge Smith watched with his head stuck out of his side cockpit window. When he saw the last grunt get on board and received the thumbs up from Stevens, he raised the collective and swung the nose away from the most intense fire. Increasing power, he watched the needle on the manifold pressure gauge climb until it almost touched the red line. He might over-boost the engine, but engines were expendable. His ass wasn't.

Five hundred meters away, just out of sight beyond a tree line, a similar rescue was taking place. Reb Johnson, Chief and Jenkins were hauling themselves up onto the skids of Lawson's hovering Huey. As soon as they had scrambled aboard, Lawson pulled pitch and shot through the curling smoke column of Reb's burning UH-1 hoping the smoke might offer some concealment. Climbing away from the wreckage, he joined up with the lumbering H-34 in a banking turn for Da Nang.

Ha-si Truong crawled out of the mud of the paddy and stood on the edge of the cemetery and watched the two departing helicopters. He had lost seven men on his side of the attack. He surveyed the damage around the temple and counted all five of the mortar's impact holes. That was how many rounds of ammunition remained from their raid on the air base three nights before. Now they had none. He hoped more would arrive from the north. It was getting increasingly difficult to steal from the ARVN, and their contacts in the South Vietnamese Army who were easily bribed were afraid to do business at the moment due to the Americans crackdown on the black market.

"Ha-si, you did well!" exclaimed Trung-'uy Phong as he walked up from the south side of the clearing.   "The imperialists have lost another helicopter," he smiled pointing over his shoulder to the smoke that could be seen over the trees.

"Yes comrade, but seven of our comrades paid with their lives," reported Truong folding his spike bayonet.

"Eight.   Trung-si Quan was taken back to the village. He was wounded, but no doubt he will die soon."

"Quan? NO!" exclaimed Truong with a look of horror. It cannot be! No! Not Quan! His mind flashed a kaleidoscope of pictures--stories around the fire at night, lessons in tracking, days in the forest learning the ways of the land.   Trung-Si

Nguyen Hoa Quan raised Truong from a small child
after a French air strike killed Truong's parents in
1954. Uncle Quan had taken him in and taught him
everything that was important for survival in a
world such as this. The days of tracking game in
the forest, and the nights of listening to Quan's
stories would never come again. Uncle Quan
always made sure there was rice in his bowl, and
clothes for him to wear. After joining the National
Liberation Front when the war in the south
demanded more soldiers, Truong had gone to great
lengths to be assigned with Uncle Quan. He was
the only family Truong had.

Quan died before Truong could return to the
tunnel beneath the village.

To Truong, the war had been political. Now
it was personal, and the American with the yellow
hair was to blame. He had been the leader of the
enemy soldiers, and called for the helicopters who
killed Quan. Truong had watched the American
move between the imperialist positions and direct
the fighting. Truong would find the American--and
kill him.

The Marine squad lay scattered in various reclining
positions on the floor of the H-34. The adrenalin of
combat was rapidly wearing off and the fatigue of
the past two days began to take its toll. Riley had to
force himself to keep his eyes open. He still had a
squad to take care of.

Stevens nudged Riley's muddy jungle boot
and nodded out the open side door. Riley could see

the big air base at Da Nang through the low hanging
scud of monsoon season. Thank God.

"Da Nang tower, this is Iron Hawk two-
niner over 327 for landing Marine ramp, over?"
requested Lieutenant Smith into his boom mike.

"Iron Hawk two-niner, Da Nang tower,
proceed as requested. Wind one-eight-five at six,
altimeter two-niner-five-zero. Traffic...flight of two
f-fours on final for active," came the young voice
over the earphones.

"Two niner, roger, out."

In a swirl of red dust, the squad jumped down from
the door of the big chopper and ran, crouching,
toward the right front. Smith and Tanaka watched
them depart and started the cooling sequence for the
big radial engine while they waited for the fuel
truck to arrive. Tanaka knew how they felt. He
also wanted to call it a day. They had been up
since 0400 hours, and this last episode had taken
everything out of him. He knew that when he
finally unstrapped and stood up to crawl out of his
window-door, his back and armpits would be
dripping with sweat. His helmet began building
heat like an oven. His feet itched. And he swore as
he wondered how in the hell an aviator could get
jungle rot. That disease should have been reserved
for the rice paddy wading grunts. He looked up to
make sure the grunts were clear and watched as one
turned and waved at the chopper crew. A thumb's
up thanks. You're welcome Marines.

"We'll hump out to Runway Road and hitch a ride to Regiment. From there, they can figure out how to get us back to the company," announced Riley, slinging his rifle.

"Why don't we hit the Air Force club first and have a couple of bottles of Tiger Piss," asked Lamb with a hopeful grin.

"No way. The last time we was there, you got us all thrown out. The Air Force likes nice neat uniforms, language and manners. None of which you got." replied Riley remembering Lamb's latest episode in a career of bar fights that everyone else had to finish.

"Aw, come on. I only been thrown outta there three or four times. I think it would be great to go in there now, in full 782 gear and covered with dried rice paddy mud. I especially think the camouflage paint on our faces would add the piece d'resistance," goaded Lamb.

"The smell alone would keep us out. Sin loi Marine," said Riley as they reached the road and flagged down the first six-by to rumble by.

Sitting in the musty darkness of the tunnel, Truong had given his task much thought. Never had he anticipated the loss of his only relative, his uncle, his father. Quan, the kindly old man. The teacher. The friend.

Truong had made up his mind. A sniper, armed with the proper weapon, would be the only one who could fight a one-man war. A sniper was independent. He selected his targets, narrowed his enemy to what lay in his sights, and eliminated him.

By the time Truong had made his decision, he had killed the American a thousand times in his mind.

"Trung-'uy, I respectfully volunteer for the sniper school. I believe I can better serve the struggle as a sniper," said Truong pushing his bowl of rice aside. He shifted his position on the floor of the dirt tunnel and lay down his chop sticks. He had no appetite since Uncle Quan had died. The old man had lived for three days, but the peritonitis from his ruptured intestine was more than their meager medical supplies could handle. He was buried in the village cemetery with Buddhist honors.

"Ha-si Truong, are you not sure that you wish to become a sniper to avenge the death of your uncle?" asked Phong.

"I wish only to become a better soldier to help in our struggle against the imperialists," Truong lied.

"Yes, yes. I understand. You realize that it is a long journey to the training camp?" said Phong, referring to the North Vietnamese Army training camp at Xuan Mai, southwest of Hanoi. This was also the army political indoctrination center. Perhaps it could be arranged for a dau tranh instructor to see that Truong was properly trained. Phong knew that the death of old Quan had affected the Ha-si greatly.

"I do not fear the journey, comrade Trung-'uy," responded the little corporal leaning back against the cool dirt wall of the tunnel.

"Then if this is what you wish, I will speak with the 'thie'u-ta, smiled Phong, referring to his major. "I am to go to a cell meeting tonight."

"I am grateful, comrade," sighed Truong. Now I must begin to think how I will be able to find the yellow haired Marine that led those dogs that were responsible for the death of Uncle Quan, thought Truong. Then when I return with the new sniper rifle, I will kill him.

Chapter Six

Captain Diem studied his reflection in the mirror and smiled to himself. His latest pair of sunglasses looked very becoming. He was indeed handsome, and he knew it. His South Vietnamese Army uniform was always impeccable, tightly tailored and pressed, and today it was fresh. He adjusted his black beret with the gold and silver badge of the 'Biet Dong Quan'--the Rangers--to a rakish angle and turned to address his American counterpart.

"Captain Gillano, I must go to the headquarters of the National Police today to interrogate a Vietcong prisoner. Is there anything you wish from Da Nang city while I am there?" he asked the Marine intelligence officer that shared his office.

"No Diem, I don't think so. I just received a radio message that there is a Marine squad coming in that just made contact out by Khuong My. Do you want to stay while I debrief them?" The swarthy Italian knew Diem wouldn't. He didn't even bother looking at him and continued to study the map on a large plywood partition in the tent.

"No, it is not necessary. I will read your report later. I am expected at the police headquarters soon," replied the short ARVN Ranger officer picking up a plastic portfolio.

Yes, he would read the report later. Diem read all the reports. In fact his portfolio held some copies of very important reports that would soon bring a handsome profit for his efforts.

Diem liked the good life. He liked beautiful ladies, good food and fine liquor. Diem also had his own set of values concerning the war. The war was going on before he was born, and would probably still be going on after he was gone. It obviously had no end, so therefore one should look at the bright side and plan accordingly. Diem found that one who was positioned at the right place could turn the war into a profitable business. His business was information. As an intelligence officer he was privy to many secret documents and sources of information. This meant a never ending supply of "product," and the demand was constant.

Diem dealt strictly in gold, precious stones, and American dollars. There were still dollars to be had on the black market, but the supply was meager since their replacement by MPC, the hated Military Payment Currency. It was designed to be replaced on an intermittent basis so that any left in the black market when the new notes came out would become worthless. Only Americans could cash in the MPC during the amnesty period, and had to explain any over-abundance of the stuff. Diem would not take MPC. Piasters were not much better. He did not trust the South Vietnamese government either, and knew that if they lost the war, the money would be worthless.

Thoughts of gold and beautiful precious stones crossed Diem's mind as he exited the office-tent into the cloudy afternoon. The rain would soon begin to pour down in a sudden gush, as it did every day to signal the usual afternoon storm that marked the last days of monsoon season. He was glad he had a canvas top on his M-151 jeep that the Americans so graciously provided.

A muddy Marine truck splashed to a halt next to his jeep. Seven haggard Marines tiredly crawled down the sides. Diem looked down at his tightly tailored tiger-stripe fatigues and checked disgustedly for traces of splashed mud. He was still clean.

Rain drops splattered against Diem's sunglasses. He took them off and put them in his pocket. As the Marines walked toward him, one removed his helmet and pulled his wet poncho off prior to entering the wooden-floored tent.

Diem noted seeing the PRC-6 walkie talkie hanging from his neck, identifying him as a squad leader. The blond Marine replaced his helmet and saluted as he passed Diem. He was the only one who showed respect for Diem's rank. Diem did not understand these Americans. If they saluted an officer, it may be because they did not like him. A salute in the wrong place would identify an officer to any watching Vietcong.

If they did not salute an officer, it may also be because they did not like him and this was a show of disrespect. In this instance, they would fall on the 'sniper' excuse for their reason to not salute.

Diem returned the blond squad leader's salute and climbed into his jeep. There was something unusual about that one. Something in his blue eyes. So young, yet with so much responsibility.

"Hey Riley.....how come you saluted that gook?" asked Lamb loud enough for Diem to hear.

"He ain't no gook, Lamb. He's a South Vietnamese Army officer, and he rates a salute," said Riley, turning to look at Lamb.

"Aw, I don't trust none of them slant-eyed rice eatin' sonofabitches," grumbled Lamb, voicing the opinion of most Americans in Vietnam. Too many times ARVN had turned out to be VC.

Diem watched the Marines enter the tent and started his jeep. At least there was one American who showed proper respect. Unusual.

The jeep lurched forward as Diem let out the clutch and disappeared down the road toward the main gate, Da Nang and more gold and jewels.

Chapter Seven

The trek north was full of many hardships. The way passed through terrain that was rugged and densely overgrown. This in itself was not all bad as it helped to hide the small group's movement from American aircraft. Many times Truong heard airplanes pass. He flinched at each shreik of jet engines, and scurried for cover at the throaty roar of the odd piston-driven A-1 that was feared even more.

The propeller airplane would fly slow and low, searching for guerrillas. When they were detected, it would attack with napalm, bombs and rockets. The Skyraider was difficult to shoot down and carried a great deal of armament. Truong prayed they would not encounter any.

Rice, monkey meat, and the occasional rat became their meals. Hungry insects attacked them constantly and poisonous snakes were always dangerously near. The walking was difficult and fatiguing, and Truong was grateful that they were traveling north with light loads. The Vietcong they passed walking south were burdoned with heavy packs and supplies strapped to bicycles.

Days and nights flowed together. Truong's every step reinforced his determination. He was restless, and bitten by the need to arrive at his destination. Therefore, his comrades suffered that much more. Truong led the march at a determined pace, allowing little rest.

His group consisted of seven Viet Conq guerillas who were traveling north for a myriad of reasons. Two were going home on leave, one was the mail carrier, returning to the north with a knapsack full of letters that he had collected for over a month in the south, and the rest were selected from their cells like Truong to attend the new sniper school. After fifteen days of traveling at night and hiding in the day, they crossed the border into North Vietnam.

Ten kilometers north of the border, they were picked up by a truck carrying bags of rice from the rural community of Nui Thu Lu. They collapsed in the back, laying on the rice bags, and watched the countryside drift by as they bounced and lurched up Highway One to the town of Dong Hoi.

From here they went their separate ways, with the new sniper students riding in old French buses filled with peasants, pigs, chickens, ducks and bicycles to Hanoi.

They decided to sneak in a few hours of sightseeing in the city and enjoy the luxuries they had missed in the south.

Truong was not as surprised as his two companions at the condition of Hanoi. He had been here on his way south from his training camp when he volunteered to join his uncle in the Viet Cong. His two new friends had never been north. Both were local farmer-Viet Cong from the area west of Da Nang.

Many buildings were rubble on the outskirts of the city, yet the city itself was intact and operating normally. How could it be that the Americans would bomb everything in the country and not bother Hanoi? wondered Truong looking out the window of the bus. He did not believe that it was entirely due to the skills of the heroic anti-aircraft gunners and missile technicians of the People's Army. He had fought the Americans enough to know that this alone would not keep them away. He remembered the helicopters of Khuong My.

"What are those round things in the sidewalk?" asked one of his southern brothers. "Are there so many rice urns here that they must put them up and down the street?"

"Those are shelters to protect the people from imperialist bombs," explained Truong.

"But I see no damage from attacks," noted the second man.

"Not yet, but we must be prepared. If the American air pirates attack, then you should jump into one of those holes and pull the concrete cover over the top to keep falling debris from hitting you," Truong pointed out.

"Let us hope it will not be so. I am weary of caves, holes and tunnels," sighed the youngest VC.

After the debriefing, the Marine squad caught a truck for a ride to Regimental Headquarters. As the truck passed the parking ramps for the airplanes, Peewee noted the unloading activities.

"Check that shit out!" exclaimed Peewee pointing to a huge stack of long green metal boxes piled next to the ramp where the cargo planes came in. "If that's ammo or weapons, there ain't much security to keep the VC from gettin' it."

"You don't have to worry about the VC messin' with those boxes. They're all empty," said Galleon.

"Yeah," laughed Slacker, "you're lookin' at one of the ways you might get outta Vietnam."

"What do you mean?" asked Peewee shoving his glasses back up on his sweaty nose.

"Those are shipping containers for body bags,"
explained Lamb. "All you gotta do is get yourself killed."

"So many? what in the hell do they need so many for? asked Peewee worriedly.

"Ain't you figured it out yet? asked Lamb sarcastically as the truck hit another bump and Lamb's helmet bounced up and slammed down on his black horn rimmed glasses, painfully shoving them into the bridge of his nose.

"Figured what out?" asked Peewee still eyeing the coffins.

"You can't take it personal. It's simply a matter of supply. There are certain things that are sent to Vietnam and certain things that are sent home. We are a supply item. We are sent to Vietnam just like ammo and equipment. We're part of a system. One rifle, one uniform, one pair of boots, one Marine. When we become unserviceable, we're sent home. Just like a worn out tank or chopper," Lamb said seriously.

"Yeah," added Galleon. "And it all depends on how 'unserviceable' you are to determine how you get home. If your time is up, you rotate home. Then after six months stateside, you're back here. If you're wounded seriously and can't come back, then you're out and that's that. If you get the 'Three Heart Rule,' the Corps figures that you've about used up all the luck God issued you. After all, if you've been wounded three times and you're still alive, it's time to ship out for permanent non-combat deployment or maybe back to the World. The last way is to get zapped. Then you fill one of those boxes. The supply people don't care which. They just order a replacement--like a spare part for a machine. You, my friend, are a spare part for a Marine rifle squad."

"One thing about it though," quipped Lamb, "at least you get to fly home."

"Fuck that! I'd rather walk than go home like that," Peewee sneered.

"Mrs. Burnett's baby boy is goin' home upright," emphasized Slacker as he pulled his poncho from his belt. It was beginning to rain.

"We're all going home in one piece, now shut up and un-ass the truck," ordered Riley as the six-by jolted to a halt in front of the Ninth Marine Regiment's headquarters area.

Major Talanin Dharkov was a Russian in name only. His grandfather had been a captain in the Soviet Navy stationed at Vladivostok. Captain Dharkov had met and married his grandmother, a Korean woman who had crossed the border to Sikhote-alin'--the finger of Siberia that juts south along the Pacifac, bordering China on the west, Korea on the south, and the Sea of Japan on the east.

They had one son, Udek, who--as his father before him--served in the Soviet Navy as a junior officer. While assigned as a navigation officer, Udek's ship became trapped in ice in the Barents sea and was crushed by the huge white arctic floes.

Lieutenant Dharkov saved his captain's life during the episode and, after being rescued by an ice breaker, was awarded the gold star on the red ribbon that is most coveted by military men. He became a Hero of the Soviet Union.

Udek returned to Vladivostok in 1932, and like his father, married a woman of Oriental background. Their son, Talanin, was born in 1933. Talanin Dharkov, having grown up in a seaport town, hated the sea. He was conscripted into the army for two years after graduating from school and elected to stay when his time was up. It was better than Siberia.

Prejudice in the Soviet Army manifested itself in many ways, and Talanin found that one who looked Oriental stood little chance of advancement in the Eurasian dominated Red Army. He enlisted the aid of his father, who still maintained good relations with his former captain, and managed to secure an appointment to Officer's Training School. The now Admiral Dobrynin had repaid his debt.

The school had been difficult, but Talanin Dharkov had managed to stay with the top of his class. Sports were a mandatory subject, and Talanin found one he excelled in-- rifle marksmanship.

He shot on the school team for four years, and after graduation, was made a marksmanship instructor in the Army Sniper School. This would last only six months.

Prejudice impeded his career after graduation. Talanin struggled through the officer ranks, serving mainly in border posts along the Sino-Soviet border, and finally North Korea.

When the Soviet Union began sending "technicians" to Vietnam, Dharkov volunteered. He was first sent to the Soviet Army Language School. English was a mandatory subject in his early school years, and Vietnamese added a third language to Dharkov's education.

The assignment in Vietnam held two promises; a way to beat the system and achieve further promotions and decorations, and a chance to get back in action. The latter was sorely missed since his departure from the 38th parallel in Korea.

Now Dharkov felt he could finally control his own fate. He sat in a thatched reed hut in North Vietnam and listened as his North Vietnamese counterpart greeted the new students.

"Ha-si Truong, you have done well. You have the highest scores in the basic classes. You will now receive your reward," said the instructor smiling. "This is Major Talanin Dharkov, of the Soviet Army," he said motioning to the muscular man who stood up from behind the table in the small grass and bamboo house that served as the school office.

"Major Dharkov is one of the finest snipers in the Red Army. He will finish your training."

The odd-looking Russian stepped around the table and Truong could see that he was wearing a strange spotted uniform. The Soviet camouflage pattern was unusual to Truong who was used to the solid colors of the Americans and the Vietcong and NVA. Truong studied the mans eyes. The eyes would tell the tale. A man who had been blooded in combat and had suffered the experiences that go along with it had a certain look.

Dharkov had cold, calculating, steely dark eyes. He did not have the dull stare of a combat veteran, but he definitely looked dangerous. Yes, this man was a killer. What Truong didn't know was that Dharkov had spent two years training North Korean Army snipers for service on the Demilitarized Zone of Korea, and had gained battlefield experience during several border "incidents". Dharkov had killed.

"It is now time to refine your skills. Soon you will be sent south to serve the revolution again," said the Soviet officer with no change of expression. "I will train you and two of your comrades. You three are the top shooters of this class. Tomorrow morning I expect to see you on the shooting range ready to learn."

"I am honored," said Truong.

Dharkov stood behind a table that was covered by a large green canvas tarpaulin. Lifting the corner, he pulled it aside, revealing three strange weapons.

The three Vietnamese students studied at the rifles with anticipation and wonder. Never had they seen such weapons as these.

"What you see before you," Dharkov began, "is the 7.62 millimeter Dragunov SVD."

Dharkov picked one up and worked the bolt. "This is the replacement for the Moison/Nagant Model 1891. It fires the improved 7.62x54 millimeter rimmed cartridge at a muzzle velocity of eight hundred and thirty meters per second. In skilled hands, it will kill with accuracy at ranges up to eight hundred meters. More than enough for the terrain you are fighting in."

"The Dragunov is a semi-automatic, gas operated rifle with a magazine capacity of ten cartridges. The operating system is the same as the AK-47, but cannot be interchanged with that weapon. It also differs in the fact that it cannot be fired fully automatic."

Pointing at the scope, Dharkov continued. "This is the PSO-1 telescopic sight. It has a magnification of four power, and has an integral reticle illumination powered by an internal battery. This sight is capable of detecting an infra-red source--in case the Americans are using such a lamp on their weapons."

Truong noted the cut-out wooden butt-stock and the incorporated pistol grip. This weapon would indeed help him in his quest.

"You will note that the barrel is much longer than the AK-47--five hundred and forty-seven millimeters in length, actually. The Dragunov weighs four point three killograms. With the tightened rifling twist of one turn in two hundred and fifty four millimeters, it is much more accurate than the AK-47 and many other special-purpose sniper rifles."

Dharkov paused, then handed the weapon to Truong.

"Here--this one is yours."

Truong took it with reverance. It felt will balanced--and deadly.

Dharkov handed the other two students their new weapons. "There are only ten of these rifles in Vietnam. I have one, each of you now has one, and the other six will be given to the three best shooters of the next two classes. If you do well in the south, more will follow."

Truong was impressed. Buddha had smiled.

After two days of shooting at static targets, the trio was assigned to moving targets that shifted from one side of the range to the other at varying speeds. Then they went to a range where man-shaped targets--each one becoming the yellow haired American to Truong--would be pulled up from the grass at different distances. This improved the range-estimation skills of the students, and their reaction time.

"You only have two seconds to shoot when the enemy raises up from a position of cover," coached Dharkov as he knelt next to Truong who lay camouflaged in a spider trap on the firing line. "You must see, estimate distance, sight and shoot in two seconds. One shot, one kill. Do you understand?"

"Yes comrade. It is very difficult," said Truong dropping the scope from his eye.

"No comrade Truong, dying is difficult. That is what will happen if you do not kill the enemy before he detects you. The secret is to kill your target at the longest range that can be engaged. The closer he gets, the more dangerous he is to the sniper," instructed Dharkov, in a tone hinting experience.

"Yes comrade, I will improve."

"I know you will, sighed Dharkov standing up. *These monkeys often amaze me at how determined they are. Of course, so are baboons,* thought Dharkov. In his Russian indoctrinated eye, no one was as intelligent as a soldier of the Soviet Army.

"I ain't short no more!" exclaimed Lance Corporal Edmonds. "I got my orders. I'm goin' back to the world!"

"No shit! You finally got your walkin' papers, huh?" asked Riley looking up from his book. Kipling was a favorite, and he had been memorizing poems from Barrack Room Ballads when Edmonds stormed into the tent.

Riley's squad had just been rotated back to the air base at Da Nang to provide security for two weeks while another battalion relieved them in the field. It was a welcome break, and afforded them the chance to get over some of their jungle rot and dysentery, and catch up on a little rest on a more routine schedule.

"I got my orders right here," grinned the lance corporal, waving a packet of papers over his head, "and I ain't even gonna look back. My girl is waitin' for me, and I got forty-five days leave comin'. All I'm gonna do is eat ice cream, guzzle ice cold beer, drink ice cold milk, and get laid," said the Edmonds while he stripped semi-dry jungle utilities from a clothes line inside the tent and threw them into his open sea bag.

"Did the Skipper say that Galleon was gonna get your team?" asked Lamb.

"Well...no, not really. There's a new guy comin' in. I don't know his name. He's down at Battalion now drawing his gear. Skipper said he's just in from gettin' wounded down at Chu Lai. He was with the 7th down there," advised Edmonds.

"That ain't fair. Toby's been waitin' for his turn and he's been here all this time. We don't even know this new guy, and he's being put in a leadership position. He might even be some boot shitbird!" protested Karlov sitting up wearily on the edge of his cot.

"Skipper said he has other plans for Galleon," said Edmonds, closing his seabag and throwing it on his cot.

"Yeah? What?," asked Riley with more than a trace of sarcasm.

"Something about Sniper School up at Division. I gotta go guys," answered Edmonds, grabbing Riley's hand. The rest of the squad that was not on guard duty or a working party lined up to wish Edmonds the best.

"Hey, any of you assholes get to Nashville, look me up." Edmonds, shouldered his seabag, waved one last time and sprung down the steps. Edmonds was now a man who could see his future.

Riley watched him disappear into the heat waves rising from the steaming ground. *Well, he made i*t, Riley thought shifting his gaze up at the darkening sky. It would rain soon....

On the last day, the Soviet officer stood before his students. "You have successfully completed your training. We have taught you everything that we can. When you came here you did not know the little tricks that will make you victorious on the battlefield. Now you do. Remember the things that you have learned here. They will both save your life, and end the enemies. You now have a challenge--a problem to solve--so to speak.

"A sniper's war is a personal thing. Often you will be alone, yet you must act and must survive to shoot again. The object is to kill the enemy efficiently, and without emotion. You have all killed before, and therefore should have no emotion.

"The remaining part of the problem is to do it efficiently, and the solution to that problem lies here," said Dharkov to his three pupils sitting together in the shade of a large teak tree.

Holding an SVD sniper's rifle over his head, the major paused for effect, then continued, "...The Dragunov Solution."

Chapter Eight

Truong poured a handful of rice into the boiling water in a tin bowl that sat on the ground before him. He was taking advantage of the twilight that casts the long shadows in the forest to hide his cooking fire. The smoke of the tiny charcoal fire he had constructed would dissipate through the leaves of the trees over his head, but even a tell-tale wisp at the right time of day against the emerald green foliage might be spotted by Yankee aircraft. Truong kept an ear cocked to the evening sounds, listening for the engines of approaching airplanes. He had heard of the devices they carried that could see in the night and detect fire and heat. If an aircraft approached, he would bury the coals with the mound of dirt that he had dug out of the hole he had built the fire in, then run to the river fifty meters distant and swim downstream. The imperialists bombs could have the rice, but not Truong.

He squatted before the glowing embers and thought of the journey. He was once again crossing the border, this time traveling south. With him were four new replacements on their way to the 40th Regiment near Chu Lai. They were young and not yet blooded in battle, sent to travel with Truong as far as the tunnel complex headquarters west of Da Nang. From there, they would continue on their own.

Truong marveled at how young they were. Han was sixteen and Thang barely seventeen. The other two appeared even younger. Their innocent faces and dark eyes watched Truong's every move. Everything he did impressed them, for he was a veteran. And he was still alive. Obviously he knew what he was doing, and they would learn from him. Troung noted their attentiveness and was pleased. He remembered what it was like to watch Uncle Quan and listen to his wisdom. Now he was the mentor. After all, he was much older than his charges--he was nineteen.

"Ha-si," said Han as he squatted next to Truong, his AK-47 resting against his shoulder ready for instant action just like Truong instructed, "what manner of weapon is that?"

"It is a Dragunov sniper rifle, comrade," answered Truong.

"I have never seen such a weapon. What is its purpose?"

"It is built to shoot great distances with accuracy," answered Truong, looking up to peer into Han's eyes with a stare that made his backbone chill. "It is a very deadly rifle."

"With such a weapon you can kill many imperialists?" asked Thang.

"Yes, many. But if I kill just one more, one particular American..." Truong started, a far away look entering his eyes, then, "But that is another story."

"Please, Ha-si, tell us the story," Han pleaded.

"No. It is not one to be told." Truong immediately regretted mentioning it aloud.

Han could see that Truong's mood had changed and decided to change the subject. "You say this rifle is called a Drag...Drag...."

"Dragunov. But I have named it Uncle Quan," replied Truong softly as he stirred the rice with a stick.

"Why did you pick that name?" persisted the young soldier.

"It is for my uncle who died in battle."

"I see," said Han, nodding his head.

No you don't, thought Truong. You do not see. Not without knowing the story.

The Marine instructor stood before the class, a bolt-action rifle with a green anodized telescopic sight cradled in his arms.

"This is the M40 sniper rifle chambered in 7.62 millimeter NATO. It fires a full metal jacket, match grade bullet at a muzzle velocity of twenty-eight hundred feet per second. With this rifle you can hit a man at eight hundred meters, and on a good day, if you're lucky, one thousand meters"

He paused for effect, then continued; "The scope is a three-by-nine variable that is field adjustable. If you can see 'em--you can kill 'em. It has three horizontal stadia lines. You line up the target with the top two lines, until he is inside from feet to head, then read the range on the 'tombstone' ranging device in the bottom of the scope. You can then adjust your elevation accordingly to that you can shoot center of mass with the crosshair reticle. We have had some trouble with the tombstone as it is made out of clear plastic, and if you aren't careful and leave the rifle leaning up against a tree or wall and the sun shines down the objective lense, it will melt the tombstone. IF than happens, just crank the scope up to nine power and leave it. That the shot and use Kentucky elevation by estimating the distance in one of the manners we will teach you."

Toby Galleon listened half-heartedly. He had not volunteered for this. And he wasn't sure exactly how he had been picked, except that the gunny had gone through the SRBs at Company headquarters and sifted out the Marines in the company that had qualified Expert at the rifle range in boot camp. There were several, but for some reason his name had been picked from the list. Either the gunny was mad at him--or liked him. He wasn't sure which.

"When you return to the field," continued the instructor, working the bolt to chamber a round," you will be able to shoot the tits off a pygmy at five hundred meters." He turned, faced the target line and took up a rest position on a make-shift shooting bench. All eyes alternated between him, the rifle and the targets.

KRACK!

An empty Bai-Mui-Bai bottle, stuck upside down on a stick in the ground five hundred meters away, exploded in a puff of glass dust.

"That, people, is accuracy," said the instructor turning to face the class. "That also is...death. In the hands of a competent sniper, it is the most cost effective weapon on the battlefield. There is nothing more deadly than the single well-aimed shot. One shot, one kill. We call it the 'thirty six cent solution'."

Galleon was impressed. Perhaps being a sniper would prove interesting after all.

"Hey Riley, Peewee and me are goin' to town and check out a steam-and-cream, wanna go?" asked Lamb jamming his wallet into his khaki trousers.

"Gunny say you could draw liberty today?" asked Riley looking up from his cot where he was writing a letter home.

"Yeah, I think the old guy likes me now."

"He would just rather have you fucking up Da Nang instead of his Marine Corps," chirped Peewee, finishing a knot on his jungle boot.

"Watch it there, feather merchant," threatened Lamb. "If I want any shit outta you I'll squeeze your head."

"Where're you guys goin'?" asked Riley, wondering if they were planning to just hit the skivvi houses in Dog Patch, outside the main gate, or go on into Da Nang where there was more action.

"Oh, we thought we'd have a few drinks at the New Chicago Cabaret, maybe get laid at a boom-boom house, then catch a cyclo down to the PX and see if they got anything worth a shit. Last time we were there, all they had was washing detergent for automatic washers, Marine Corps rings and nylon hose. Now what the fuck do you think they use that nylon hose for over here anyway?" asked Lamb.

"Maybe they sell it to the gooks to make fish nets for leeches," offered Murphy, who was just rousing from his cot in the corner of the tent.

"You finally decide to join the land of the living?" joked Riley. Murphy had slept more than ten hours since returning from a night ambush patrol.

"Fuckin' 'A', man. I don't wanna miss any of the action if you shitbirds are goin' to town."

"Well, you pukes go ahead. I gotta stay here and stand by for the word on those new rifles," said Riley as he wiped sweat from his eyes with a towel.

"Yeah, I heard. The word is that the doggies down south have had those M-16's for a while now and that they are some really bizarre shit," said Murphy. "I heard that all you gotta do to clean them is hold them under water and empty a magazine on full auto!"

"That ain't shit, man," interjected Peewee. "I got it from a guy in Delta company, who has a cousin in the Army, that if a bullet from an M-16 hits a man in the finger, it will tear his whole fucking arm off."

"I think that's a load of crap," said Eddie Karlov, joining the conversation. "But I heard that the bullet tumbles in flight, and when it hits you, it bounces around inside your body bustin' everything up until it expends its energy."

Riley shook his head. "I don't know man. I'd just like to keep my M-14. It ain't never let me down." He had heard other, not so glamorous stories about the M-16. There had been too many reports of mysterious jamming associated with the new design.

"Yeah, but now you gotta draw a forty-five. You're a squad leader and squad leaders carry pistols," said Karlov.

"Yeah, I know. I sure hate giving up my M-14 though. As I said, it ain't never let me down...."

"Comrades, this is where we part," said Truong as they came to a fork in the jungle path. "We have traveled far and I wish you luck in your future."

"Thank you comrade Truong," answered young Han. "You have been of great help and we have learned much from you. May you and Uncle Quan find happiness and victory."

"And may Buddha smile on you, binh-nhi Han. And remember what I said. You must all work together and look out for one another. Do not take anything for granted, and do not trust anyone until you know them well. That is how you stay alive in this war."

The young soldiers smiled, shouldered their weapons and turned away. Truong watched the four privates walk down the shady path until they disappeared in the shadows of the forest. Once they were gone, he opened the camouflaged cover of a tunnel entrance and dropped in. Tonight he would rest after the long journey. Tomorrow he would begin to test his new skills. And his new weapon.

Chapter Nine

The sun was beginning to set over the mountains in the west. Truong knew that he had only a short period of time to accomplish his task before the tropical night closed down like a window shade over the world. The Americans could be seen moving around near their bunkers and holes behind the spiked wire that they depended on for protection. Truong knew that the Viet Cong had many sappers that could cross through the rolled wire slowly but efficiently whenever they chose. They simply wore only shorts or even removed all their clothes and often coated their bodies with oil. They would part the wire and slip quietly through in the darkness, carrying cloth sacks of explosives to strike the imperialists.

This day the wire would not protect the Yankees. This day "Uncle Quan" would breath the fire of the dragon. Truong closed his eyes and rested for a moment.   He had been watching the Marines through the scope for several hours. He had narrowed his choice of targets down to two men who often exposed themselves by standing up in plain view near their bunker. His plan was simple; he would take the one with no shirt first. This one was sitting near the door of the sand bag house. When his companion ran back to the house to aid his comrade, "Uncle Quan" would take him too. Truong knew that the Yankees would return fire, but it would be inaccurate since they did not know where he was. Many Imperialist bullets would be wasted shooting trees and shadows.   Truong had been trained well, and he knew that after taking the two Americans, he must move to a new place.

Truong pulled the Dragunov up to his shoulder in a relaxed prone position and brought the scope to his rested eye. The illuminated post in the center of the scope moved across the landscape as he slowly panned the weapon across the scene in front of him. There he was--his first victim. This time would be for practice. It was not yet time to avenge the death of his uncle.

"Hey Murdock, you wanna trade some 'ham, sliced and fried' for some 'beanie-weenies'?" asked the young Marine private sitting on an ammo box near the command bunker.

"Naw, I hate that shit. If you have any pogey-bait from home I might be interested."

"I ain't got a care package in a month, man."

"Whatta I gotta do? Write your girlfriend again?" asked the Marine named Murdock with a grin.

"Go ahead an' write her. Maybe you can get a better response than I can for care packages. Hell, she's probably racked out with a squid now anyway, And I don't wanna compete with the whole Pacific Fleet," said the big Marine with the name "J.B. Brixley" stamped over his pocket.

"You don't have to. Just any sailor named Jodey," laughed Murdock as he began opening a can of c-rations with his P-38 c-rat can opener hanging on his dog tags.

Brixley picked up his poncho and shook it out in preparation for the night. They would be on fifty percent alert again, and he had the second watch. At least he could get about four hours sleep before Murdock would wake him up. This perimeter guard duty sucked. He would be glad to get back to the air base for some down-time.

"Hey Brix...you got an extra..."

Murdock never finished the sentence. Brixley looked at him just in time to see his shirtless back erupt in a red volcano and his body slam backwards to the ground. Then he heard the shot.

"Incoming! Incoming!" yelled Brixley as he ran to the aid of his buddy. "Corpsman! Corpsman...DOC!..."

Brixley never heard the second shot.

Truong slid back into the brush in the stand of sugar cane while the American bullets buzzed through the foliage seeking revenge. He would give them a few minutes and allow the fire to cease before he would act again. Truong slithered like a snake into a small drainage ditch and managed to crawl more than a hundred meters before the air was silent again. There was just enough light left for one more victim.

"Get me a Med-evac on the horn, and tell 'em there ain't no hurry," said the Captain in the bunker. He had two KIA's for pick-up. He hardly knew Brixley, but he'd known Murdock since they left the States. Murdock was a good man, thought the Captain. He was always cheerful and made a good brunt for practical jokes by the other men. Having him around was good for morale. Now he was gone. The Captain looked through the firing port of the bunker and saw the muddy jungle boots of the two Marines sticking out from beneath the green rubber ponchos that covered their still bodies. A stab of sadness mixed with a feeling of failure came over him. Was he responsible for their deaths? Could he, as their leader, have done something different? Questions. Too many questions. Too much responsibility.

"Sir! Another man was just hit on the right side of the perimeter."

"Another sniper?" asked the skipper of the gunnery sergeant who had just hung up the EE-8 field phone.

"Yes sir, there must be two of 'em. Second platoon is sending out a fire team to try and get him."

"Who got hit?"

"Corporal Perkins...machine gunner," said the Gunny,
picking up his rifle.

"Where you goin'?" asked the Captain.

"Better get my ass over to that machine gun position 'case they try any shit."

The Captain listened as the fire died down from that side of the perimeter and wondered if they had seen any targets or were just shooting out of frustration. He knew that the platoon sergeants and platoon leaders would be yelling cease-fire by now. The Vietcong had only fired three or four rounds. His people probably spent a couple of thousand dollars worth of the taxpayers brass.

The Captain went outside the bunker and squatted down next to the two dead men and pulled back the ponchos to say goodbye.

"Jesus...that gook sniper was either one hell of a shot or the luckiest sonofabitch in the world. Look at this," said the Captain.

The Gunny turned and came back to where the officer squatted in the dirt. "He never felt it, Skipper. Right in the ten ring."

The Captain closed Murdock's sightless staring eyes and covered him with the poncho. "I don't think we was a lucky shot, Gunny. I think we got problems."

"That ain't no shit," said the stocky gunnery sergeant as they both looked at Brixley's body. Brixley was unrecognizable. There was a gaping hole where his nose used to be.

"Right between the runnin' lights, Skipper. I never saw a gook that could shoot that good."

"Pass the word for everyone to keep their asses down. I want some ambush patrols out tonight. I want that sonofabitch!"

But Truong was gone.

Chapter Ten

"You better tank up on that beer," Lamb said to his three buddies sitting around the table in the bar. "I got the word that we're goin' back out to the field in a couple of days."

"Yeah, I heard," said Karlov. "Too bad Galleon ain't here to help reduce papa-san's stock."

"I don't think that we'll be able to reduce it much. I think he makes this stuff in the back and just uses the bottles over and over," chirped Peewee holding his bottle of Tiger Piss up to the light. "I wonder if that is really shit that's floating around in this stuff?"

"Of course. That's how they make it ferment quick so they can get it on the shelf for thirsty gyrenes," smirked Murphy, pushing Peewee's bottle back down to the table.

"That's disgusting," moaned Peewee spitting on the floor.

"Name one thing in this shitty country that ain't," sneered Karlov as he turned to mama-san to order another round.

"How's that 'Remington Raider' Williams doin' with his war souvenir business?" asked Lamb referring to the company clerk who sold anything he could get from the line grunts to the Air Force at the air base for a tidy profit.

"I heard he was doin' pretty good.   He's got a special this week on captured VC battle flags and NVA dog tags," Murphy informed his mates.

"The NVA ain't got no dog tags," said Karlov.

"Yeah, but the wing-wipers don't know that. He has them punched out of aluminum and puts gook names and numbers on them. Some dink on Doc Lap Street makes 'em up for him," said Murphy.

"Where does he get all the VC flags?" asked Peewee.

"He's got a mama-san on the payroll down in Dog Patch who makes 'em. Then he takes 'em out and stomps 'em into the dirt to frazzle them up. Sometimes he even shoots a few holes in them to go along with whatever story he makes up on how they got captured in some big firefight. The zoomies don't care, all they want is something to take home to tell war stories over."

"Think we could sell him a few SKS's and AK's?" asked Karlov.

"He said he could move anything we could bring in. The market's wide open. I heard that some of the Air Force pukes turn around and sell this shit to other flyboys in Guam and the Philippines," answered Murphy setting down another empty bottle.

"Hell, we oughta sell all our crap to the Navy. They don't ever get near the real war and I bet they would pay premium price for authentic captured stuff," said the Mad Russian.

"Only problem with that is we ain't out of the field enough to make contact with the squids," said Lamb.

"Yeah, I guess some guys have all the luck," laughed Murphy picking up a fresh bottle.

Galleon did not consider himself especially lucky. Much of his down time was being used up in sniper school. He volunteered to be a sniper once, but changed his mind later. He really didn't want a bolt-action rifle. He liked a weapon that fired on full automatic when you squeezed the trigger. He didn't care how accurate it was, he wanted to put some heavy "rock-and-roll" into the bush when he needed to.   Screw surgical accuracy.   His philosophy what that if you put a lot of shit downrange and you were bound to hit something.

Terms like boiling mirage and bullet drop and the "minute of angle" rule didn't impress him. Most of his experience in Vietnam had proven that his targets normally would be less than a hundred meters. What the hell would he do with a scope?

But in the Marine Corps it didn't matter what you wanted, it was what the Corps told you to do.

"Alright people," said the chief instructor, "file by the truck and draw your ammo. This is the real thing and it's time to get out to the field a become heart-breakers and name-takers."

Toby got in line in the hot sun and picked up five boxes of match grade thirty caliber full jacketed ball ammunition. He carefully put the twenty round cardboard boxes in his pack and squinted toward the dusty road. His truck would arrive shortly to take him and the other snipers to their assignments. He wondered where his would be.   He would miss Riley, Lamb and the rest.

Sergeant Alexander stuck his head in the doorway of Riley's tent.   "Hey Riley, diddy-bop down to Supply and see the armorer about your squad's weapons turn in."

"Yeah, okay. I sure hate to give up the '14's though."

"You ain't giving up no M-14. The Skipper told me to tell you to draw a forty-five. He said all his squad leaders are gonna carry their T.O. weapon."

"I'll remember that when I gotta beat some gook to death with it 'cause I couldn't hit him, or it jammed," moaned Riley disgustedly as he pulled on his jungle boots.

"Tell 'em you want a bayonet stud welded to it and you can scare the shit out of 'em when you jump outta the bush," laughed Alexander. turning away from the tent.

"I see you ain't got no forty-five," Riley yelled as he watched the Right Guide move off toward the next squad tent.

Riley found the armorer opening green wooden crates with a crow bar outside the battalion supply hut. "You got our new miracle weapons ready to issue?"

"Any time your people are ready," he answered looking up. Two other privates in his working party were busy pulling black metal and plastic M-16s out of the open boxes and laying them out on a large canvas sheet spread on the ground. Riley picked one up and examined it. It was the first one he had ever held.

"This thing is definitely light," he said hefting the short odd looking weapon.

"Yeah, and the cartridges are somethin' to behold. I used to shoot rabbits with bigger bullets," the armorer exaggerated.

"Je-zus," exclaimed Riley picking up a bandoleer of ammo and extracting a clip of the small rounds. "What caliber is this stuff?"

"Five point five six millimeter. Supposed to be some really bizarre shit. They say that you can carry enough of it to never run out."

"I hope you're right. I don't like my people going to the field with something that hasn't proven itself in combat," Riley said, replacing the clip in the green cloth bandoleer.

"The army has been using it for a while, and they've had a few problems--jamming and such--but they've probably got it worked out now," said the armorer moving to a new crate.

Riley looked the rifle over. It felt about half as heavy at his trusty M-14, and had a carrying handle on top with the rear sight enclosed in the rear of the handle. The stocks were plastic, and would not need to be linseed oiled like the wooden stocks of the M-14. "How the hell do you butt stroke someone with this thing?" he asked tapping the hollow plastic butt stock.

"Very carefully buddy, very carefully."

"Eddie, I got an idea. I read a book once about some dude in World War Two that used to contract with the Germans to bomb his own air base. We could contract with the VC to shoot our own people!" shouted Lamb over the roar of the six-by that was taking them back to the company area.

"Are you for real man?" questioned Karlov in an equally loud voice.

"Well, the book was fiction, but the idea might work."

"Anybody ever told you that you were full of shit?" asked Murphy.

"Each and every day of my life, man. No shit though, we could take turns being the target. All we gotta do is this--when we come back from a patrol, have one guy out in the open in the perimeter and one of us in the patrol shoots over his head and he falls down like he's been hit. Just like in the movies. All we need are some good actors. The VC think we shot someone, and leave some cash in a box someplace for us to pick up later. They leave us alone 'cause we're doin' their work for them and nobody gets hurt and we get rich."

"You are definitely full of shit, Lamb. I think that what they really oughta think about is laying asphalt all over this stinking country. Make it one huge parking lot. We could contract out the construction work with the Seabees and engineers and hold the profit margin for ourselves. No more tunnels or bunker complexes, no more mine fields and no more rice paddies," said Murphy with mock seriousness.

"Yeah, but then the Air Force would be out of a job. They wouldn't have anything to bomb," said Lamb in defense of his plan.

"Oh they could go ahead and bomb the parking lot if they want and we could contract to repair the pot holes. We could even pay them to create pot holes so we could get paid to repair them," answered the Mad Russian.

"I got a better idea," said Peewee who up until now had remained silent. "Let's contract with the VC to rent us their tunnels and we can pass the word state-side to the hippies that we are selling stock in opium mines !"

Lamb thought about this for a moment. "Opium don't come from mines. It grows on plants, stupid."

"You know that, and I know that, but do all the hippies know that?" asked Peewee shoving his glasses back up on his nose.

"Well, we might sell a few shares..."

Truong had chosen his position carefully. He had found a rocky outcropping overlooking the small bridge over the Song Con river where the Yankee soldiers pumped their water into large round rubber tanks. He had watched their movements carefully since the sun had risen. Now it was time. He picked up Uncle Quan and placed the wooden stock to his cheek. The safety lever clicked down exposing the slot for the bolt handle to retract in and he took aim. The lone guard on the bridge stopped to light a cigarette. As he exhaled the first puff of smoke, his head exploded with the impact of the Dragunov bullet.

Marines threw themselves to the ground and grabbed at their weapons. Truong could see the look of confusion on their faces through the scope.

He shifted to his next target. He had the advantage of the high ground and he could easily see the Americans scrambling for cover from their various positions. The breath of the dragon reached out once more and a prone figure rose slightly off the ground with a jerk. Not a clean shot, but effective. Now it was time to move again.

"Alright people, it's time to get the new rifles. Let's move out and get it over with," said Riley with a tone of disgust in his voice.

"Okay by me," said little Peewee who had no lost love for the heavy M-14. "The Corps finally got smart and got a weapon for ME!"

"Nobody ever accused the Corps of bein' smart," Riley said, while strapping on his pistol belt. "I'd be more than happy to give you this piece of shit," he added pulling the old worn-out forty-five automatic from the black leather holster. He held it up, dropped the magazine out of the handle and retracted the slide to clear the chamber. Letting the slide slam forward, Riley held it up to his ear and shook it. It rattled. "I can see I gotta carry more grenades."

The squad turned in the M-14's with mixed emotions. They had grown to love the wood and steel rifles. The Corps had taught them well. Murphy remembered the words of his Drill Instructor in boot camp; "While you are here, I am your mother, your father, your sister and your brother. But...this rifle is your best friend! You take care of it and it will take care of you. You fail it and it will fail you. Learn to love this weapon.

Remember--the deadliest weapon in the world in a United States Marine with a rifle!"

The voice of the battalion supply sergeant broke his daydreaming. "You guys hat up and make it over to the road. A six-by will pick you up and take you to the range for fam-fire. They got some instructors there waiting to teach you guys how to shoot."

"That guy is a ton of laughs," sneered Lamb slinging the little black rifle over his shoulder as the squad turned toward the road.

"Yeah, too bad he don't have to go to the field with us and see if we ever learned how to shoot," added Karlov.

Captain Gillano stuck another pin in the casualty map and turned to Major Strebor. "The way it adds up, we got us a gook sniper that can shoot. He started out here," he said jabbing a finger at the map, "...and progressed steadily south to here, where he hit two more troops yesterday."

"What makes you think this is all the same sniper? I imagine the VC have a lot of snipers," asked the major, peering over Gillano's shoulder at the map.

"Us super-spooks here in intelligence examine what we call a modus-operandi just like the police do back home. This guy only shoots two people, then moves out. He never hits the same location twice and he never misses. He usually tries for the head or heart. The ranges he shoots are in excess of what an AK or an SKS will hit with any accuracy. And the speed that he can engage multiple targets is much higher than he could with a bolt-action

Moison-Nagant sniper rifle. We don't know what he has, but it's obviously an auto-loader, and damned accurate."

Gillano walked over to the map. "He either strikes just after dawn or just before dusk, but always at twilight. Each incident occurs a day apart, and the distances are what a man can move on foot in one day if he is moving slowly. We think it's the same sniper, and he's working his way around the enclave perimeter toward the south. I suggest we set up ambush patrols, here--and here, for the next two nights," said Gillano pointing to two locations on the map.

"I think you've got an active imagination, but I'll see what I can do. What do you think Diem?", asked Strebor, turning toward the Vietnamese officer.

"It is possible. But as you say, many snipers could have the same training and act the same way. The VC are very disciplined and will do exactly what they are told to do. If they are trained to only shoot twice and then leave, then that is what they will do," answered Diem, cleaning his sunglasses once again. It seemed that he was always cleaning something. Gillano had never seen him dirty, or sweaty, or tired. Gillano was growing to dislike Diem.

"Well, let's get the word out that something is going on. I don't think it's possible for any of the VC to be this good with the old trash sniper rifles that they have. Most of them are rusty old hulks with shot-out barrels. Something different is definitely happening," cautioned Gillano. He had that old gut feeling that he was right, and he wished he could ensure that every man on the perimeter would keep his ass down until they found out what was going on.

Chapter Eleven

Tanaka closed the cowling of the big Pratt and Whitney on the H-34 and wiped his hands on a rag. "Hey Smudger, everything checks okay here," he yelled up to Smith in the cockpit who was going over the pre-start check list.

"Okay Tanaka, how's the Chief doing?"

Tanaka looked around the right side of the machine and replied, "Just about loaded up. You ready up there?"

"'Bout five. Looks like another milk run. I hope that oil pressure holds up. I get real paranoid watchin' that gauge all the time."

"If it don't, we'll be instant grunts!" laughed Tanaka, somewhat nervously.

Five minutes later the big radial engine belched into action, blowing smoke out of the exhaust stacks as the lower cylinders cleared of oil. It soon settled to a steady roar and the huge rotor blades spun up to a ragged blur.

"Mister Smith?" asked Danny Stevens through the ICS system.

"Yeah Chief, you ready?"

"No sir, not yet. Could you hold for just a couple of minutes? I'll tell when to go and when I give the word, pull pitch fast and get us outta here, okay?"

Tanaka and Smudger looked at each other and wondered what Danny was up to now. Every time you turned around it seemed like these enlisted types pulled some kind of shit. Tanaka looked out his side window toward the rear of the ship in time to see an off-duty ARVN soldier pedal up to the side of the helicopter on a bicycle and stop at the door.

Danny looked down at the smiling ARVN who was holding up a cardboard sheet filled with watches.

"YOU BUY?" yelled the South Vietnamese over the roar of the engine.

"WHAT?" Danny feigned ignorance.

"YOU BUY SAME-SAME NUMBAH ONE WATCH?"

"LET ME SEE," screamed Danny as he grabbed the whole sheet full of the cheap time pieces. He acted like he was examining them while he keyed the intercom and spoke into the mike, "Let's get the hell outta here!"

"Hang on Danny, here we go." Smudge pulled up on the collective stick and coaxed the heavy machine into a hover.

The ARVN soldier waved his arms in the air and screamed something in Vietnamese at the departing helicopter. The wind blew his boonie hat off and sailed it across the ramp. He began to pedal his bicycle furiously after the airborne machine as Danny watched, grinning. The Sikorsky gained altitude. None of the watches were worth a shit, and this dude had been ripping off the new guys with outrageous prices for months. Danny had bought a watch from him for five hundred pi when he arrived in Vietnam, and it quit working that night. The watch vendor would not give his money back and Danny vowed revenge. The helicopter turned back over the flight line and took up a southwesterly heading. As they passed over the Vietnamese straddling his bicycle at the end of the apron, Danny stripped the watches off the cardboard and tossed them out the door. They splattered all around the ARVN, who promptly threw his bicycle down and began to pick up rocks to throw at the helicopter. By then it was too high and too far away. He threw the rocks down, picked up his bike and pedaled away.

"Numbah ten GIs!" he mumbled. "Numbah ten sixty-nine thou GIs!"

Ha-si Nguyen Van Truong had spent the entire night infiltrating the Marine perimeter to gain access to Marble Mountain. From the crevice in the face of the high cliff, he had a commanding view of what the Americans called the Marble Mountain Air Facility and the South China Sea beyond. The Yankees felt safe here. They had built a hospital across the road and down the road further, sailors could be seen working on heavy equipment in another compound. There were many targets, and he would be hard to find. But Truong was here for only one target; the helicopter that had snatched the yellow haired Marine from his grasp at Khuong My. He had waited until the sun illuminated the eastern sky, and when there was enough light he scanned the parked green machines with his scope. He found it sitting in line with the others just as he expected. The number on the tail was the same that had burned into his memory during the fire fight many weeks before.

One hour after the sun came up, three men had approached the helicopter and began walking around, poking at this and shaking that. It appeared to Truong that they were preparing to fly. Truong watched the South Vietnamese government puppet pedal up to the machine, and then chase the helicopter as it took off. Truong wondered mildly what that was all about, but did not allow the small mystery to break his concentration. The machine and its crew were too far away for an accurate shot, so Truong had no choice but to wait.

Truong's faith in the smile of Buddha proved justified as he watched the lumbering noisy giant insect turn and fly straight toward him. This may be the only chance he had. He must try for the pilot. If that failed, he would attempt to injure the machine.

Just as the helicopter came abreast of him, rising toward the clouds, he sighted in on the cockpit. He could clearly see the pilot, and he took up the slack on the trigger while he allowed a lead on the moving craft. That is when it happened.

Truong did not know that the mountains of marble were also the home of several tribes of rock apes. Truong also did not know that the rock apes are very territorial and became jealous of any and all intruders, Truong not excepted.

Splat!

Truong recoiled as something warm hit his face, surprising him. He jerked the shot off and it went wild, not even noticed by the crew on the helicopter. Truong rolled to his side and clawed at the stinking deposit on his face. Shit! He did not know yet what had happened, but he suspected it was some kind of Yankee trap. He rolled quickly onto his back, looked up and brought the Dragunov to bear for a snap shot at the ambusher. Then when he saw them. Three rock apes, very large and very irate. They chattered back and forth, then to him. The leader was a large old male with gray chin whiskers. Truong laughed with relief. He did not know how dangerous rock apes were, but he did know that they were not as dangerous as Marines.

"Very well done, grandfather," said Truong to the old ape. "You have the right to be angry. I have invaded your home like the imperialists have invaded mine. You are also an excellent shot, so from one excellent shot to another I will give you the courtesy of life. You may live today, and may the great Buddha smile on you and your people."

Truong noted the gray chin whiskers on the old one and named him "Ho" after the patriot Ho Chi Minh. Truong's bestowing of honor did not impress the old ape, for he was busy gathering more shit.

"Hey you boots, quit your grinnin' and grab your linen. The Marine Corps' secret weapon is back!" shouted Toby Galleon, walking up to the truck that was preparing to depart from the tent camp area with his old squad aboard. He had just barely made the convoy before it left, and had run as fast as his load would allow down the line of trucks on the dusty road to find his platoon.

"Well Je-zus Ke-rist, if it ain't the 'Colorado Shadow', ol' Spanish Galleon hisself," mocked Foster looking over the tailgate at the swarthy Marine. "Is that your new bullet launcher?"

"Yeah, and I see you got a new piece too," replied Galleon as he crawled up the side of the six-by, using the large tires as a ladder.

"Piece of shit, you mean."

"Looks like we're back to muzzle loaders and toy guns. Hell of a way to fight a war," grinned Galleon, squeezing in between Lamb and Thomas, who still had his M-60 machine gun.

"Yeah, you guys oughta pay me extra for covering your asses with my trusty ol' chopper," said Thomas patting his gun. Thomas liked to refer to machine guns as "choppers" after growing up on a steady diet of gangster movies.

"Just don't forget whose asses you're covering," said Riley with a frown. He still wasn't happy with the fact that he now had to carry a pistol. He pulled a map out of the cargo pocket of his jungle utility trousers and unfolded it on his lap. "Toby, are you going with us?"

"That's affirm-a-titty, brother. I lucked out and got assigned back to this battalion with my partner, Mendoza. He's back down the line a few trucks riding with his old squad in Kilo company, but he'll off-load with us. I swapped a couple of chi-com baseballs to a clerk back at Battalion for the assignment to this company, and here I am."

"What does Mendoza do?" asked Riley.

"He's my spotter. His job is to find targets for me and my shooter here," answered Galleon holding up the M40 sniper rifle for all to see.

Lamb eyeballed the rifle. "Is that thing as accurate as they say?"

"Pretty damned accurate. It can put three rounds into a shot group the size of a quarter at two hundred meters if you fire from a rest position," said Galleon seriously. He wasn't crazy about the bolt action, but he had become impressed by the accuracy.

"Well, one thing for sure, you and me ain't gonna do any bayonet fighting," said Riley.

"Why do you say that?"

"A weapon just ain't a weapon if it ain't got a bayonet stud."

"You tryin' to make me think you were in the Old Corps or somethin'?" grinned Galleon.

"Sonny, I was in the 'crotch' when you were still shittin' green down your diapered ass," Riley shot back. Galleon and Riley were in the same platoon in boot camp, but Riley had arrived at Marine Corps Recruit Depot two days before Galleon and waited in Receiving Barracks for his series to form. This made Galleon boot to him and Riley never let him forget it.

"Well, for an old salt, you look pretty young, lad!" Toby was twenty, Riley nineteen. Galleon never let him forget that.

Darkness came and Truong moved the brush he had cut as camouflage away from his crevice. He scanned the American bunker line along the edge of the helicopter place and quickly found his prey. An American was walking along the fence line apparently on guard duty. Truong let his image center in his scope and took a breath. He relaxed and squeezed the trigger. The Yankee spun and fell into the wire in a heap, his weapon tumbling to the ground. Another heart shot. Truong slid quietly back into the bush and faded away.

Chapter Twelve

The trucks lurched to a halt in a cloud of dust outside An Hoa, a small town twenty-two kilometers southwest of Da Nang. Riley looked around and saw Sergeant Alexander walking down the line of six-bys.

"Alright ladies, un-ass the trucks. We ain't got all day. It's time to hump again," Alexander yelled as he marched by toward the head of the column. John Wayne would have been proud of Alexander, thought Riley. The guy is for real, and Riley wondered if the Corps knew he existed. Yes, Alexander was part of a dying breed. He was born twenty years too late to be appreciated.

The squad crawled heavily down the side of the truck and formed up at the side of the road in anticipation for the march to their new base camp. They were relieving another company that had been positioned in a company patrol base somewhere northwest of An Hoa. Word had it that this area was hot with activity, and the number of home-made mines and booby traps was out of sight.

Galleon's spotter, Mendoza, came shuffling up under the weight of a full packboard. Galleon watched him approach, and as soon as he caught up, did the honors. "This is Corporal Riley, squad leader of the second squad," said Galleon introducing Jeff. "These bedraggled bastards are the rest of the squad. Thomas is our gunner and this is his 'A' gunner Darryl Simmons," he nodded toward the Mutt and Jeff team.

Simmons had just returned from the hospital after his leg had healed following the action at Khuong My. He continued to introduce the rest of the squad and ended with Lamb who asked, "Mendoza? Is that a Russian name?"

"Lamb is our resident idiot," explained Galleon.

"Aw, come on man. I'm just on the lookout for a buddy for Karlov. He ain't got no friends," said Lamb in mock indignation.   "Bullshit Lamb, I had a friend once," said the Mad Russian slinging his rifle.

"What happened to him?" asked Lamb in anticipation of a set-up.

"He found out you were in this platoon, and that's the last I ever saw of him."

The company began moving out in a ragged column and within minutes changed course for the interior. The men automatically formed a tactical staggered column when they left the road. Riley could see the long whip antenna up ahead marking the Captain's position. He could mentally see the little form of PFC Martin, the company radio man.

Martin would be bent over under the weight of the PRC-25 trying to keep up with the Skipper. Martin reminded Riley of a dog on a leash. He could be seen trailing behind the Captain with the mike cord to the handset stretched forward to the Ol' Man while he talked. When "Actual", which was the call sign extender for the commander, was finished with his transmission, he would toss the handset over his shoulder and Martin would have to catch it. If Martin was not paying close attention, the black plastic handset would sail back and strike him. Martin always wore his helmet.

The terrain around this new place was different than any that they had operated in before. It was deep dirty-white sand that swallowed each footstep, making the going tedious and causing the muscles in their calves and ankles to ache. The only vegetation in sight was several short evergreen trees. It reminded Riley of a huge Christmas Tree lot that had mistakenly been planted on a wide beach. The short hairs on the back of Riley's neck began to tingle with that old feeling. This would be an ideal spot for snipers. They could hide behind any little tree that they wanted and change positions at will. Not good.

"Where was all this sand when we were filling sandbags at the air base?" asked Foster. "We sure coulda used it then."

"Foster, I hate to tell you this, but the Commandant just had this sand delivered yesterday. I wrote him a letter and complained about having to patrol in rice paddies and asked for some dry land instead. He saw the light and sent this stuff over from Camp Pendleton just for me," Riley bantered.

"Why the hell would he do that for you?" asked Foster.

"'Cause the Commandant and me are old surfin' buddies, that's why," explained Riley with a grin. "I thought everyone knew that."

"Riley...did anyone ever tell you that you were full of shit?"

"No, but I got the word that Lamb was full of shit."

Foster thought about this for a moment then replied, "You and Lamb are full of shit."

"Knock off the shit back here, ladies," ordered Alexander, who had stopped near a sand dune to watch the column go by and monitor the interval. "You're supposed to be Marines, so spread it out and stay alert. If you got up this morning with the intent to piss me off, you're beginning to succeed. There's a goddamn war going on here, this ain't no walk in the sun."

"Alexander's full of shit, too," mumbled Lamb.

"I heard that, Lamb!"

"Je-zus."

The company base camp area north of An Hoa was not an impressive sight. It was built on a wide hillock of sand, little more than a huge dune, and did not appear to be the world's greatest defensive position. Though it was the only "high" ground in the vicinity, the crest was barely over fifty meters above the surrounding terrain. Two sandbagged bunkers were located at the top, one at each end of the long hill. Riley could see a single radio antenna thrust up from the bunker on the right. Obviously the command bunker.

At the base of the hill, near a break in the concertina wire that served as a gate, a small abandoned Buddhist temple embellished with carved dragons on the crest of the tile roof sat between two scraggly palm trees. There were marks of bullet strikes on the concrete walls and many of the dragons were missing body parts. The temple had been taken over by one of the platoons that had preceded them and was presently being used as the platoon command post. WD-1 commo wire led from it to the command bunker and out to each squad CP position. Between the small one room temple and the command post, just before the rise of ground, an 81 millimeter mortar pit had been dug and the crew was busy disassembling their weapon. They appeared only too glad to be leaving this place.

"First Platoon...crap out behind the temple until we get the word where we'll be," ordered Staff Sergeant Hays. The Lieutenant broke away from the platoon and hurried up the hill to catch up with the Company Commander.

"That hump was a sonofabitch," gripped Slacker, letting his packboard fall to the ground.

"Every hump is a sonofabitch," added Lamb.

"Yeah, but at least we got here with dry feet. My feet ain't been dry since I been in this shitty country. I got so much jungle rot I gotta use Agent

Orange to kill it," spat Karlov as he collapsed onto the ground in the shade of the temple wall.

"I hear that, man. Agent Orange has a double O number with a license to kill," said Thomas who had read every James Bond book he could find.

"Just don't use that stuff on your crotch if you get crotch rot," advised Riley following the banter.

"Oh yeah? Why not?" asked Lamb.

"One morning you'll stand up and your dick will fall off Lamb looked at him in mock indignation. "So what? I ain't using it for nothing now anyhow."

The platoon moved to their assigned positions in the heat of the noon-day sun, occupying the fighting holes of the weary grunts of the relieved company. Thomas emplaced his M-60 to cover the gate, laid out his right and left limit stakes and adjusted his traverse and elevation device for the correct deflection to cover the ground to his front at waist high level. He checked it by traversing his weapon. Satisfied, he pulled an empty c-ration fruit can from his packboard and began making instant coffee. Just as the muddy looking liquid started to steam, the Lieutenant came by and said, "Thomas, you and Simmons move about twenty-five meters to the right and dig in."

"Move sir? We just got here..."

"I know, but I gotta have this position for the 3.5 team," explained the platoon commander.

"But sir, them rockets never work, and the VC ain't got no tanks anyway, and this is the best position for the gun, and..."

"Just get your gear and move, Marine. Last time I checked, I was in charge here," ordered the Lieutenant, beginning to lose his patience in the heat.

"Yes sir." Thomas grumbled as the Lieutenant moved off down the line to check other positions. "It never fails. The fuckin' rocket team just sits around on their fuckin' asses waiting for us to dig a hole, or get set up, then they tell the fuckin' lieutenant that they need our position. The lazy bastards ain't dug a hole since we fuckin' landed. They just keep taking ours. Every damned time we get comfortable we gotta move. Why in the hell don't they just fuckin' leave us alone?"

"Because officers get paid to fuck with us, that's why," answered Simmons, picking up the tripod.

"I wish someone got paid to fuck with them!" Thomas spat back as he shouldered the machine gun.

"They get fucked with too," said Simmons.

"Oh yeah? by who?"

"Other officers, man. Captains fuck over lieutenants, majors fuck over captains and colonels fuck over majors and so on up the line," explained Simmons.

"Where does it all stop?"

"With the Commandant of the Marine Corps, he fucks over everybody!"

"Then we got it made," laughed Thomas, slapping Simmons on the back.

"How's that?" he asked.

"We know Riley."

"So?"

"Riley and the Commandant are ol' surfin' buddies," explained Thomas.

"Bullshit."

"No bullshit G.I. Where do you think all this sand came from? Biggest goddamn beach in the fuckin' world!"

The tunnel was dark and cool. Truong felt relaxed for the first time in weeks. He had reported back to the Trung-uy after his excursion to Marble Mountain, and had been given permission for a well-deserved rest. Uncle Quan lay peacefully by his side and he stroked the wooden stock gently like one would a well-loved pet. Truong thought back to the nights and days of waiting without moving that went with his mission. He likened himself to a cobra that hid in the shadows until an unwary victim came by. Then the cobra would strike. The cobra was very patient. So was Truong.

Truong had reported his kills. Twenty-three. Faithful Uncle Quan never missed. His spirit lived the in wood and steel, and Truong knew that he was never alone when he had the Dragunov. The old Vietminh sergeant was always with him.

Tomorrow, he would receive his new orders. The place of operations would change, and he would have to go out again. This would aid Truong in his quest. The Trung-uy did not know it, but Truong had been searching for the yellow-haired Marine each day. But there were too many Americans here. He discovered that it would be very difficult to locate the killer of his uncle. Truong tried not to think of the possibility that the

Marine had left Vietnam. Surely Buddha would not allow that to happen before Truong could exact his vengeance.

Trung-uy Phong had promised Truong a day in Da Nang as his reward for his victories. In two days, he would infiltrate the imperialist defenses like he and many other Vietcong had done in the past to visit the city. He simply had to carry a "student" Cuan-cuk identity card and dress in western clothes. He would cross the big Phong Le bridge that spanned the Cao Do river with the peasants going to market. He would smile at the guards, and they would merely watch as he walked by. How simple.

Truong had heard that one could find out anything one wanted to know from certain contacts in Da Nang. All it took was money. Truong did not have much money, and even less of the South Vietnamese dong, but he did have some gold and a few small jewels that his family had passed along to him. Now that he was the only member left of his family, the heirlooms meant little. They would be well spent if he could use them to locate the yellow-haired one. Only two things held meaning to Truong now: the Dragunov--and his vendetta.

The young Vietcong lay back against the cool earth and closed his eyes.

Chapter Thirteen

The rains of November pelted down, beating a dull tattoo on the helmets and hooches of the weary Marines. Nothing was dry. Water soaked every piece of clothing and equipment.   It rusted everything made of steel, making it a constant job to wipe down, clean and oil the weapons to keep them serviceable. The only saving grace was the fact that the sand soaked up much of the water, and it did not cling to the troops and vehicles like the mud of the rice paddies farther north.

Christmas was just around the corner, but it seemed light-years away for the men who knew that each day might be their last. Each man in Vietnam who was exposed to the dangers of combat every day hardened themselves to the constant task of living each day as it came. Survival was the issue, and survival became an art. Those replacements who came as individuals and joined the units one at a time had the advantage of having experienced people in their squads and platoons who could teach them and give advice. This began to happen once the "boot" was accepted by the "salts". If a new replacement was a shitbird, then he was on his own. One had to learn to fit in, or lose any advantage of the experiences of others who came before him.

Private   Rawlings,   Richard   R.,   was   a replacement. He arrived one day like a spare part for the rifle squad. An otter--an unarmored tracked vehicle more at home in the snow than the tropics--

arrived escorted by three M-48 tanks who had been assigned to the base camp, and once safely inside the perimeter, disgorged five gallon cans of water, several cases of small arms ammo and 81 millimeter mortar rounds, two orange nylon sacks of mail, and Rawlings.

Unlike the rest of the Marines who originally landed with the battalion, Rawlings was not a volunteer. He had not joined the Marines, he had been one of the first to be drafted into the Corps. His Drill Instructors hated him and the other draftees, because they could no longer use the old Marine come-back during recruit training; "Nobody twisted your arm, asshole, you volunteered to be here."

After standing alone in the driving rain for a few minutes wondering what to do next, he noticed the small temple near the gate. It looked like a good place to get out of the rain and he was in no hurry to do anything else.

The porch roof of the temple was supported by narrow concrete columns that had pieces of commo wire strung between them to serve as clothes lines. Damp green utilities hung limply from the wire, and Rawlings wondered how long they would take to dry in the wet air. This was Rawlings' fourth day in Vietnam.

On the ground outside the doorway were stacked boxes of ammo, grenades and C-Rations. Rawlings shrugged out of his pack and let it fall to the ground. He noted that most of the grunts he had seen wore the canvas and wood packboards, and wondered when he would get one. The regulation canvas

World War Two knapsack was uncomfortable and didn't hold very much. He had been told that he would be updated on equipment once he got his permanent assignment. This was it.

"You the new replacement?" came the voice from inside the building.

Rawlings looked in and tried to make his eyes adjust to the darkness. "I'm Private Rawlings."

"Come on in, lad," ordered the voice in the dark. Rawlings, Richard R. entered and tried to approach the figure on the far side of the room, but stumbled over someone on the floor.

"Hey! Watchit shitbird," came the sleepy epithet from the prone body wrapped in a poncho.

"Sorry, uh...anybody know where I'm supposed to report?"

"You're here.   I'm Staff Sergeant Hays, the platoon sergeant. The Lieutenant is up at the CP gettin' briefed by the Skipper for our next operation. You'll be assigned to Riley's squad. Grab your gear and report to him. He'll show you where to set in. After that, we'll see about gettin' you some 'Nam seven-eighty-two gear. Keep your eyes and ears open and your mouth shut and you'll get along fine. You'll find Riley's pukes down the line that way," said Hays, pointing down the string of fighting holes and bunkers. "Just look for a sign that doesn't belong in Vietnam. That's them. Any questions?"

"No sarge, not yet."

"Rawlings...this ain't the goddamn Army, and I ain't no sarge. I'm a Staff Sergeant, and you'd best remember the proper terminology when addressing Marines. We may be in Vietnam, but we're still

Marines.   Discipline is the key to survival in combat,   and   this   is   a   disciplined   outfit. Understand?"

"I understand," answered Rawlings, realizing he had already screwed up. He knew enough not to want to bring attention to himself, to keep a low profile, but had already failed in that. And he'd only been here ten minutes.

His eyes had now adjusted to the dim light of the temple, and he managed to thread his way out to the porch where he picked up his pack. He slogged down the line until he came to a sandbagged fighting position with a homemade sign on a stick stuck in the sand outside the wall that announced "Los Angeles City Limits."

Riley and Galleon were sitting inside under the protection of two suspended ponchos reading mail from home. Rawlings stuck his head in and asked, "Is this second squad?"

"Depends on who wants to know?" said Riley.

"I'm a replacement. Staff Sergeant Hays told me to report to Riley," said the New Guy.

"Then this is second squad," said Jeff looking up from his letter. "Come on in and have a seat."

Rawlings dropped his pack and pulled it into the hole after him. "Where do I find Riley?"

"It's Corporal Riley, and you just found him," said Galleon nodding at the squad leader.

"I   thought   sergeants   were   squad   leaders," Rawlings mentioned as he sat down.

"In the real world, that's true. We got a shortage of sergeants here," advised Riley.

"Yeah, but he ought to make three stripes this month if all goes well," continued Galleon folding up his letter and putting it in a small plastic bag with other letters that had been read many times, and would be reread over and over again.

"You guys seen much action?" came the standard question asked by new arrivals.

"Well, I'll put it this way, We used to have sergeants, and not all of them went home upright," answered Galleon.

"Do the VC pick out the leaders?" queried the replacement.

"The VC pick out anybody they can hit. They especially like boot privates," replied the Coloradan with veiled morbid humor.

"Like me?"

"Like you."

Riley waited for Galleon to have his fun before speaking. "My job is to keep you alive. Your job is to do what you're told to do, when you're told to do it. I am going to say one word, and I want you to remember it. Death. Don't ever forget that word. I want it to hit you right between the runnin' lights like a sledge hammer. I want you to see the 'light'...the white light, the eternal light, the guiding light. The light that casts shadows. The light of enlightenment. The light of knowledge. I can only keep you alive if you do exactly as I say. Galleon....give him the nevers."

Rawlings young face turned to Galleon. "The nevers are things that you never do! Never walk closer than ten meters from the guy in front of you. Never cough or sneeze in the field. Never stand still and look around. Never go on patrol with a weapon you haven't cleaned and checked. Never go to sleep on watch, and above all, Never forget the nevers!" Galleon looked at Riley. "How about the always?"

"Yeah," nodded Riley. "Tell him."

Galleon held up one fist and with each statement, extended a finger. "Always wear camo paint on an operation. Always carry two canteens, and keep them full. Always know what to do if we're hit. Always tape or tie down all loose gear, and jump up and down to see if any still rattles. Luke can hear a rattle, or a slosh of a half empty canteen long before you get near him. And above all, Always watch your team leader and do exactly what he tells you to do. Any questions?"

"Yes...uh..who's Luke?" asked Rawlings.

"Luke the Gook. If he can hear you, smell you, or see you, he can kill you," said Riley.

"Sure hope I can remember all that." Rawlings rubbed his chin.

"If you can't, we'll send you home," said Riley.

"Home?"

"In a body bag."

Lamb, Karlov and Foster walked up and dropped cases of c-rations and ammo on the ground. They had been to the CP for the supply run.

"This the boot?" asked Lamb.

"Yeah. Rawlings," said Galleon.

Lamb grinned and turned to his companions. "We better give him the traditional welcome."

The three got together and hummed a long note. Satisfied with the key, they began;

"You're goin' home in a body bag, do-dah, do-dah,

You're goin' home in a body bag, oh dah-do-dah-day...

Shot between the eyes...shot between the thighs...

We'll send you home in a body bag, oh dah-do-dah-day-y."

What a welcome, thought Rawlings.

It had been easy for Truong to enter Da Nang. The Marines guarding the bridge hardly noticed the young Vietnamese among the groups of peasants and farmers who were heading to market with their baskets and animals.

Once in the city, he avoided Doc Lap street and headed directly away from the river front where most of the Americans frequented the bars and restaurants. He knew that they were not permitted to venture more than three streets away from the river, and Truong knew that he would be safe if he avoided that part of the city.

Comrade Phuoc had told him once that he could always find revolutionary sympathizers at a certain house next to a cabaret called the "Golden Tiger". He followed the directions and found the cabaret without difficulty. It had been several months since he had see his friend, and was not sure that the house was still safe to approach, so he crossed the street to a sidewalk cafe and found a table from which he could watch the from. A waiter stopped briefly and he ordered rice and nuoc-mam fish sauce.

For almost an hour he watched the front of the building, a two story French colonial house with peeling wooden shutters open to the tropic air. The rain had finally stopped, and Truong watched with amusement as the Citroen automobiles and motorbikes splashed water on the pedestrians who had once again began to fill the sidewalks.

He would wait until dark, then he would cross the street and see if the people who lived in the house could help him in his quest.

"We'll put you with Pete Longarrow, he's three holes down. You can't miss him," instructed Riley.

"Longarrow? Must be some kind of indian," said Rawlings looking down the line.

"Mohawk. He don't talk much, but he has his shit together in a small bag. Just don't give him anything to drink. He gets kind of crazy when he hits the alchohol," advised Galleon.

"What do you mean crazy?" asked the boot.

"Oh, nothin' much. He just takes scalps and such, you know... silly old indian shit," said Riley with a serious face.

"You mean VC scalps?"

"Not necessarily, lad. Not necessarily."

Chapter Fourteen

When Truong arrived at the old man's house for the meeting, Diem was already there. Truong was ushered quickly inside and taken to a small room at the rear of the house where he was offered a chair. Diem sat across a table quietly smoking a smelly Vietnamese cigarette. Truong noted that even though the room was dimly lit, the South Vietnamese officer wore sunglasses.

"I understand that you seek some assistance," said Diem matter-of-factly.

"Yes, I am looking for information," answered Truong, sitting down.

"And how may I be of help?" queried Diem, exhaling a cloud of blue smoke that lingered over the table.

"There is a man--an American--I seek."

"And why do you seek him?" Diem crushed out his cigarette in a small marble ashtray carved in the shape of an elephant.

"That is not important. I understand that you have ways to find out certain things, and I am willing to pay for this knowledge." Truong already did not like, nor trust Diem. Anyone who would sell out his friends for a price, may also sell out his customers. Truong would be careful.

"And what is the name of this...American...you seek?"

"This I do not know. That is one of the things that you must find out," said Truong.

"You do not give me much information to work from. How am I supposed to find this man with nothing to go on?" asked Diem while mentally calculating how much he should charge for this service.

"I know this--on the tenth of September this man and his squad ambushed five of my comrades near a village called An Trach. After that, they left and attempted to escape. I tracked them to Khuong My where we trapped them. They would be dead today but for the helicopters that snatched them from our grasp. During the fight I saw the man I seek. He had dropped his helmet and I saw that he had yellow hair. He appeared to be the leader, and he ran from one spot to another giving orders to the others," explained Truong, consciously leaving out the death of his uncle.

"So you wish to avenge the death of your five comrades," smiled Diem lighting another cigarette.

Truong also smiled. If that is the answer that the Captain wants, then so be it.

"What else can you tell me?" Diem continued.

"The helicopter that saved them had a number on it's side. This is the number." Truong slid a small scrap of paper across the table. Diem picked it up and examined it.

"Ah...that will be of help," smiled Diem sitting back in his chair. "Yes, I believe we can do business. Do you have money?"

"I have this to start. I will give you more when we meet again, provided you have answers to my questions." Truong placed a gold necklace with a jade medallion on the table.

"We will meet here in one week," advised Diem, taking the necklace. "I may know something by then." Diem thought of the golden haired Marine that saluted him that day in September, and wondered if it could be one-and-the-same. No, that would be too easy.

Major Talanin Dharkov was a happy man. After his fifth request, he had been given permission from Moscow to travel to South Vietnam to continue his mission. He had argued that it was much more effective for one man to go to the students, than it was for many students to come to one man. This was his justification, but not his reason. He missed combat, and was weary of training these monkeys with little reward for his efforts. He would send his students south, and seldom hear how well they did. He had secured permission from his Vietnamese counterparts to travel to South Vietnam to "evaluate" his former students, and train new snipers. With their added pressure on Moscow, which had been hesitant to allow a Russian to be close to the combat for political reasons, Dharkov had finally been given permission--provided he dress as a North Vietnamese soldier. His Oriental features finally paid off, greatly easing Moscow's concern.

"Comrade Dharkov...I must warn you that Moscow is very concerned with the repercussions that may occur if you are caught by the imperialists," said Colonel Boris Yelenkov, Dharkov's immediate Russian superior in the Security Section of the Russian consulate.

"I am aware of the Directorate's concern," nodded the Major with a feigned look of seriousness.

"Then you understand it is imperative that you are not captured?" emphasized Yelenkov.

"I will not be captured, comrade."

"I hope not, for your sake, Major. Remember, you are not to participate in any actions, and while in the south, you will appear and act as a Vietnamese. Is that understood?" said the Colonel as his eyes studied Dharkov's for any sign of deceit.

"I understand," said Dharkov.

"I cannot emphasize enough that you must stay away from any danger. The upcoming offensive that will take place on the TET New Year will, how shall I say, disturb the bees in their own nest?"

"Do not fear, comrade Colonel. I do not wish to become 'stung'," smiled Dharkov.

"Then I wish you a good journey, and when you return I may be able to arrange a visit home." The Colonel stood to shake Dharkov's hand. Dharkov stood to attention, shook the Colonel's hand and snapped a salute. The meeting was over.

Dharkov walked into the street and thought of the Colonel's words. Home? Dharkov's home was where Dharkov was at any given time. He had no great fondness for Moscow, or Vietnam, or Korea. He only had a fondness for action.

The lieutenant had returned from his meeting at the CP and briefed the platoon on the mission. It was a standard Search and Destroy operation. The name had been changed due to the media attention on the wording of this type of operation. Now it was known as a Sweep and Clear. It was the same thing, but the wolf now wore sheep's clothing. It was still a wolf.

Two hours before dawn, two platoons had climbed on tanks and left the base camp for a drop-off point some two "klicks" out. Once there, they would form a temporary patrol base and coordinate with the other companies that had done the same thing. When all were in place, the companies would move to a pre-designated location and form up on line to sweep a village complex that intelligence had said was a Vietcong stronghold.

It was nothing new, and Riley wondered if there would be anything there. Intelligence had been wrong before. If the S-2 people said that there was a regiment reported in the area, it usually meant a squad or platoon. If they said there was no "reported" activity, then look out.

"Who's going to be the blocking force?" asked Galleon over the roar of the tank engine as they lurched out the gate.

"Ain't got any. The village we're gonna search is bordered by a river, and we're going to sweep toward the river bank. There's supposed to be helicopter gunships to watch the river," informed Riley.

"That's just great. I guess Division never found out the VC have tunnel entrances underwater on the banks," sneered Galleon.

"Yeah, the generals don't come out to the field much to find out these little tid-bits of info," Riley understated.

"They outta send those navy Seals up the river and have them check out the banks before we start in," yelled Lamb from his seat on the bustle rack behind the tank's turret.

"What? Navy? Are you kiddin'? Everyone knows the Marines motto is 'First to Fight'! I mean, how would it look?" joked Karlov.

"Fuck a bunch of mottos!" spat Galleon.

The salt-and-pepper team of Midnight Lawson and Reb Johnson drew the cover mission for the sweep at Tranh Binh. It would be a controlled situation, with the Marines already on the ground in force. All they had to do was watch the river side of the village for retreating guerrillas. Lawson thought it was a bit of overkill, but he didn't make the assignments--he just took them as they came. The rain-filled clouds would keep them flying low, and Midnight didn't like this. He would rather be able to make his runs in while Reb covered him from above, then climb for the safety of altitude while Reb ran a race-track pattern and dove in for a follow-up. Today would be tree line tight.

Reb's UH-1 was in the lead and was the first to spot the bend in the river that marked their reporting position. "Bayonet three-niner, this is Silver Lance four-zero, over?"

"This is Bayonet three-niner, I have a copy. How do you read, over?" came the scratchy voice of a grunt on a PRC-25.

"I copy you lima charlie. We are in position and awaiting further, over?" keyed Reb.

"Understand in position, roger, out."

The two Hueys began a slow circle far enough away from the village complex so as not to be detected by any resident Vietcong until the Marines had begun their sweep.

"Toby...take your ass over to the right flank and set up to cover that field. I'll send Karlov with you and Mendoza. You see anybody coming from a pajama party, zap their ass," instructed Sergeant Alexander.

In five minutes Galleon and Mendoza were in position. Mendoza scanned the open area with his binoculars. "Looks like you got a clear shot all the way to that one stand of bamboo near the river."

Galleon filled a small sandbag, took his helmet off and placed the sandbag on it for a rifle rest. He donned his billed softcover to shade his eyes and took up a prone firing position. He drew the M40 to his cheek, scoped the terrain to his front and noted only two places a target might find cover. He made a mental note of their ranges and locations. It was dead calm, and the sun was low on the eastern horizon and would be no factor. By the time the company moved into the village, the sun would rise higher, reducing the long shadows and making range estimation easier. The conditions were ideal.

"Toby, let me take a look," begged Karlov.

"Okay, but don't fuck with the knobs," instructed Galleon rolling away from the rifle.

Karlov positioned himself behind the makeshift rest and pulled the scope to his eye. He slowly scanned the distant bamboo and noted how hard it was to keep the weapon on target. Each breath moved the sight picture, and every nervous twitch and jerk moved the weapon off target.

"You really gotta be steady with this, don't you?" he stated more than asked.

"It takes practice, man. Let's just hope I can do it for real when 'Luke' appears," said Toby.

"'Fraid you won't be able to shoot the bastard if you can see him up close?" goaded Karlov, laying the rifle back down.

"No, just afraid that if I miss with the first shot I might lose him. I have to take my eyes away from the scope to work the bolt, and if the VC gets spooked and hides...."

"That's what I'm here for," said Mendoza blowing minute particles of dust off the lenses of his binoculars. "I'll tell Toby where the dude ran to and then he can watch that spot until the ca-ca cabeza pokes his head up, eh amigo?"

"Yeah, then we'll put a world of hurt on the little nephew of Uncle Ho," answered Galleon turning the bill of his cap around to clear the scope. "At twenty-seven hundred and fifty feet per second."

The Marines moved forward on line and entered the edge of the quiet village. Peasants stayed close to their grass houses and the smoke of charcoal cooking fires drifted in the air. So far, so good. No sign of VC, and even the usual punji traps were no greater in number than any other ville the Marines had searched. Riley could hear the "wop-wop" of the two Hueys as they ran up and down the river behind the village. It was good to know that they were there.

"Hey, check this shit out," said Foster probing the ground around a rice urn with his fixed bayonet.

"Whattaya got?" asked Riley moving over to where Foster knelt.

Foster carefully dug around something that was buried in the hard ground and exposed a wooden box with Chinese markings.

"Watch it man, it could be rigged," said Lamb who stopped short of the scene.

"Gimme the rope," instructed Riley. Lamb gave him a fifty-foot line that they carried for just such a purpose. Riley tied it to the hinged lid of the box, fed it out until they could hide in a nearby depression, and pulled.

Nothing happened. They counted slowly to ten and Riley stood up and cautiously approached the box. "No shit," he said out loud.

The Marines looked down in the box and found several items of interest. The first thing that caught Riley's eye was a Tokarev pistol. Riley picked it up and examined it. It had a red star emblazoned on the grips. It would make a good souvenir. Foster probed the rest of the contents of the box and found two "chicom baseball" grenades, four magazines for an AK-47 and a map case containing several documents, a notebook and a map.

"Get this shit to the Lieutenant mo-skoshe, it looks important," instructed Riley, handing the map case to Lamb.

After removing all the contents of the box, Rawlings, who had been silently standing by watching the activities, reached down to pick up the container.

"Freeze" yelled Riley.

Rawlings froze, scared shitless.

"Don't ever touch anything if you don't know what it is without checking it out first!" commanded Riley sternly. He motioned the team back to the depression and made sure the rope was still securely attached to the box. After joining the others in the depression he yelled, "FIRE IN THE HOLE...FIRE IN THE HOLE..." then yanked the rope.

Dirt clods and dust filled the air as the home-made mine exploded. When the box had been jerked out of the hole, the pressure sensitive "mouse trap" detonator slammed shut and set off a large gourd full of powder, broken glass, nails and bits of wire.

"How did you know that would happen?" asked Rawlings, with an ashen face.

"I didn't."

"Hey Midnight, did you see that?" asked Reb as he banked his ship into a tight right turn.

"Yeah, wonder what it was?" Lawson responded, trying to see better past the windshield wipers that were busy brushing the rain aside. It had just begun to sprinkle large droplets, and the bases of the clouds forced the two helicopters even lower.

"Some kind of explosion. Didn't look like incoming though," said Johnson.

"Well, something is starting to happen. I'm arming my rockets just in case," advised Midnight.

"I hope we don't need them. We'll be working in pretty tight to the grunts if they get any closer to the river," said Reb.

"If they get any closer, you'll have to use guns. I'll be out of it."

The first indication of an enemy presence vested itself when a sniper in spider hole took a shot at Slacker Burdett. Slacker's padded shoulder caught the grazing bullet as the first few layers of his flak jacket burst, sending a small puff of dust into the air next to his face. Slacker was spun around with a jerk, and immediately fell to the ground seeking cover.

"Are you hit?" called Murphy who was ten meters to the left of Burdett.

"Yeah man, I think so...no, wait!" Slacker yelled excitedly. He felt under his plated jacket and pulled his hand out clean. No blood. "He just dinged my jacket!" Slacker, like all Marines, hated the hot, cumbersome flak jackets that they were required to wear on "heavy" combat missions. Slacker bitched about the jackets more than most, but then Slacker bitched about everything. Slacker liked his jacket now.

"Did you see where the shot came from?" asked Riley running up in a crouch and hitting the deck next to Slacker.

"Yeah, spider hole over there," pointed Burdett. "I gotta report that gook to the N.A.A.C.P. He definitely must be prejudiced against this splib."

"Bullshit, Slacker. I bet he would just as soon shoot a white boy," grinned Riley with relief: one of his men skated out on getting hit.

"Say what? Look at this pretty face, Riley. Can you imagine anyone wanting to shoot someone with a beautiful face like this?"

"I dunno, beauty is in the eyes of the beholder. Nobody ever told that gook that you were pretty. Let's fuck up his day," Riley rose to one knee to scope the tree line. "Peewee...Foster...cover me!" Riley ran forward and quickly found the camouflaged entrance to the spider hole. He checked it quickly and pulled it up, revealing the entrance to a tunnel.

Peewee and Foster positioned themselves on either side and took up firing positions covering the hole with their M-16's. Foster fired a burst into the dark tunnel and Peewee tossed in a grenade. They rolled away, and after the KA-WHUMP of the explosion blew dirt out of the entrance, they looked at Riley.

"We're getting close to the river. Looks like we better check it out."

"Somehow I knew you were gonna say that," replied Peewee.

"I can't help it if your mama raised a midget," Riley grinned. Being the smallest man in the squad, Peewee always drew the dirty work of being a "tunnel rat".

Peewee stripped off his gear and handed Riley his rifle. He accepted Riley's pistol, opened his pack and retrieved a green plastic G.I. issue flashlight. A good Catholic, Peewee said a silent prayer, crossed himself and slid into the opening feet first.

"Be careful, man," said Foster who knew that if anything happened to Peewee, he would fall into the category of "smallest man in the squad" and inherit his job.

Peewee felt around the edges of the tunnel for trip wires and punji pits, and when satisfied that the entrance was clear, crawled about ten meters and stopped long enough for his eyes to adjust to the darkness. The dark, cool air was filled with the smell of damp earth and mildew. He kept the flashlight off and hoped he was not silhouetted against the opening. The tunnel took an immediate ninety degree turn to the left. Peewee lit the flashlight and played its beam down the corridor. Nothing.

He turned the light off and slid the safety off the pistol. Inch by inch he crawled down the cool dark passageway. He stopped frequently and held his breath to listen. He would be able to hear more than he could see. This was not Peewee's first tunnel. After ten minutes of progress, he came to a room that was large enough to stand in. Inside were four bamboo Vietnamese beds and a few hammocks. This was evidently living quarters. Several bloody dressings lay scattered in one corner, and in the center was a cooking fire with embers still glowing. Peewee wondered how long the VC had been gone. He hoped a long time.

Three tunnels branched out from this room, and he picked the one that appeared to have been used the most. Crawling in, he inched his way for another fifty meters. His knees were getting sore, and he was anxious to find an exit. It felt like the

walls were beginning to close in. He remembered
once when he was a kid when his uncle took him to
explore some ruins in the face of a cliff in Arizona.
He had fun playing hide-and-seek with his cousins
in the old passages. Now the VC were playing hide
and seek with him, and the game could prove
deadly.

Making another turn, the tunnel descended for
fifteen meters to another level. The tunnel complex
was larger than he had expected, and Peewee started
to feel very alone. He came to another crossroads
where two side tunnels branched out. They probably
went to other spider holes, and Peewee would be
only too glad to find one. The hot sun would be a
welcome sight.

Then he heard it. A slight hissing sound. He
held his breath. What was that? It sounded like a
wounded man sucking in his last breath. But it
wasn't. Peewee froze just as something brushed his
hand. He was not alone.

He squinted his eyes in the dark and tried to
make out what was moving in the tunnel with him.
As he stared into the darkness he saw what
appeared to be two eyes staring back at him. They
were small eyes that glowed golden as they passed
through the dim light cast by one of the side
tunnels. Peewee slowly raised the pistol, rocked
quietly back to his haunches and lit the flashlight
with his other hand.

A cobra!

The large snake had made the tunnel complex
his home, and had found a little-used section of

tunnel to live in. Now there was an intruder, and the reptile stood poised to guard his territory.

Peewee knew that if he made a sudden move, he would die. Peewee hated snakes. In Arizona, rattlesnakes were common, and he had grown up listening to stories of what to do in case you were bitten by one. A cobra was ten times worse than a rattler, and Peewee only knew that he was not to move. What would his grandfather do in this predicament?

The huge snake appeared to be eight to ten feet long and had a hood eight inches across. It was not coiled to strike like a rattler, but retracted in an "S" pattern like a compressed leaf spring. The head rocked slowly right and left atop two feet of thick body, the tongue flicking from its mouth sensing the air.

Peewee decided that he must escape and leave the snake alone. He hoped the snake would allow him to do that. Should he drop his gun hand or his flashlight? He had to use one hand to support himself as he scooted backwards, but if it was the wrong hand....

Slowly, moving ever so carefully, he began drop the hand that held the flashlight and noticed the reptile follow the beam with his lidless stare. He stopped. That's it! I'll leave the flashlight on to keep the snake occupied while I get the hell out of here, thought Peewee. He placed the light on the floor of the tunnel and pushed it slowly away from his body. The snake followed his movement just as Peewee hoped. Just as he withdrew his hand, the snake struck. The flashlight bounced away from the force of the blow and Peewee fired five shots in the direction of the cobra. As fast as he could, he scooted backwards, bouncing off the walls. He had inadvertently moved into a branch tunnel that was too small to turn around. His ears rang painfully from the blast of the forty-five, but that was the last thing on his mind. He could not see if the snake was chasing him or not, but imagined the worst.

The cobra watched Peewee retreat, and slithered after him. Light began to infuse the tunnel and Peewee could see the snake plainly. Adrenalin continued to shoot through his system and he crawled backwards even faster, knocking large chunks of dirt off the walls as he went.

Just as the snake got within striking distance again, Peewee felt himself fall into a pool of water. Can cobras swim? Peewee hoped not. He swam backwards, clutching the pistol, and saw that the pool was lighted from the outside. An escape route! Peewee held his breath and swam out the opening to the river. Thank God!

Just as he bobbed to the surface outside the river bank, he saw a Huey helicopter turn and start a dive toward him. A wave of relief overwhelmed him as he found himself once again in friendly company.

"Four-zero, I got a target in the river. I'm rollin' in and rollin' hot," Reb called over the radio to Midnight.

"Roger, got you covered. Looks like the grunts flushed one," Lawson replied.

Reb nosed the Huey over and lined the floating figure up in his sight. He took up the slack in the trigger switch and was ready to put a burst of 7.62 millimeter into the water when the figure waved his hands at the chopper.

"He wants to surrender," advised Chief Whitehorse.

"Fuck him," said Reb continuing the gun run.

Just then the figure crawled out onto the bank and Chief could see that he was wearing green trousers. "Hold your fire, Reb, it's a Marine!"

Reb banked the Huey away and did a pedal turn while lowering the collective stick. He came to a hover over the surface of the river, still not convinced, and watched as Peewee turned and waved.

"Jesus. He was almost history. Wonder where the hell he came from?" sighed Johnson.

"I dunno, let's stick around until his buddies catch up with him."

"There you are, Toby," said Mendoza excitedly. "Target at eleven o'clock and he's armed!"

Galleon shifted the M40 to the left and picked up the running VC. He was carrying an SKS and was doing his best to leave the village. Toby sighted in and held his breath. Mentally Galleon gave himself the shooter's commands, breath, relax, aim...slack...SQUEEZE! The rifle jumped with the recoil of the thirty caliber round as it discharged. The small man in black flipped over backwards, throwing his weapon in air. Toby quickly worked the bolt and chambered a fresh round, ejecting the hot spent cartridge.

Karlov rose to one knee and sighted his M-16 on the spot where the VC went down. No movement. He lowered his rifle. "Let's go get him."

Just then, the figure got back up and tried to limp drunkenly to the safety of the trees. Karlov raised his M-16 and fired a burst at the moving Vietnamese. The range was too great, and the rounds went wide. He tried again and his weapon jammed. The bolt seized halfway to the rear after the first round and refused to rechamber. "Shit!" yelled Karlov trying to work the "T" handle. It had no effect.

The Marines were soon to learn that the new M-16's were suffering from mechanical defects-- weapons jamming and other malfunctions would soon become commonplace. Until the discrepancies could be corrected, many Americans would die, their weapons inoperable.

While Karlov tried to clear his rifle, Galleon took aim again. Just as he took up the slack on the trigger, the VC fell. This time he stayed down.

The sweep was over. The Marines once again boarded the tanks for the ride home, the helicopters departed when they became low on fuel, and the cobra went back to its den.

Chapter Fifteen

Major Dharkov had not imagined the hardships that he would encounter during the journey south. The trails and paths were primitive, and roads almost non-existent. The network of trails that snaked their way along the borders of Laos and Cambodia into the south brought to mind an old Russian proverb often muttered in Siberia: "This may not be Hell, but you can see it from here." The stifling heat, the steamy humidity, the pungent odor of rotting vegetation and the darkness of the canopied jungle was very depressing. Still, it hid the supply columns that funneled arms, rice and replacements into the war zone quite effectively. And he wouldn't be on the trail network for long. Only a few short days would pass before he would be out into the wastelands of Quang Tri Province, and he would travel no further south than was necessary for his mission.

On the fifth day, they had been attacked by aircraft. The American F-4's had dropped bombs and napalm on a truck marshaling point only one kilometer distant. If the attack had occurred thirty minutes later, Dharkov's group would have been there for a rest stop.

Dharkov began to see what the "monkeys" had to suffer. The filth, the insects and the diseases that attacked one's body in the tropical rain forest manifested themselves each and every hour of the journey. Food consisted of only a bowl of rice and possibly a little meat from rodents caught in the jungle. Dharkov did not ask what the meat was, but he had heard stories that the meat of monkey was often substituted with rat. Dharkov was beginning to gain more respect for his Vietnamese counterparts.

Hardships notwithstanding, the small group made good time. In twelve days, Dharkov had arrived at the Vietcong Central Committee headquarters in Thua Thien province. From there he was assigned an escort to take him to the 6th North Vietnamese Army Regiment headquartered near Duong Pham, outside Hue City. He already knew of the upcoming plans for the TET New Years holiday, and knew that this area is where he wanted to be. He was taken to a well camouflaged underground bunker complex and given a bamboo bed and a candle-lamp. As he unpacked and sorted his equipment, a young NVA officer approached and asked, "I see that you come with more than just a pistol."

"Why do you say that?" asked Dharkov.

"In the past the people who were sent to be observers were armed with only the Tokarev pistol for self-defense. I see you have brought something else," smiled the young officer, nodding toward the long green canvas bundle tied to the Major's pack frame.

"I am an instructor. I teach marksmanship, and this is the rifle I use when I instruct," explained the Russian truthfully. It is also the rifle I use to kill.

"I see. I am Thieu-'uy Vinh. I am to take you with me when I go to join my company. We have an important role in the upcoming attack on Hue, and I am told that you will observe our snipers' actions."

"Yes, I am to report on our training techniques and the effectiveness of your snipers. Especially those which were trained in the North and issued the Dragunov SVD."

"You will be welcome with us, comrade. We leave in the morning," smiled the thieu-'uy.

"Good!" said Dharkov looking up, "It will be good to...uh...see how well your men do."

Danny Stevens began to wonder if this had been a good idea. He had not been this hot since he had been in Vietnam. His package had arrived just in time from home, and his plan was unfolding according to schedule. Now, as he loaded the bulging mailbags containing Christmas mail and packages into the helicopter for delivery to the grunts in the company and battalion base camps, he sweated profusely.

It wasn't any wonder. The clothes he now wore were not designed for Vietnam. In fact the tailors had originally had someplace much colder in mind.

"Chief...what the hell are you wearin'?" asked Tanaka as he walked up to the machine.

Danny pulled the white beard down so he could speak and replied, "My arctic jungle utilities, sir."

"Aren't you taking this Christmas stuff a bit far?" asked Tanaka as he eyed the Santa Claus in combat boots standing before him.

"Just thought I would give the grunts a little better holiday, sir. Wouldn't you like your Christmas presents delivered by ol' Santa?"

"Chief...." said Tanaka.

"Yes sir?"

"Santa rides a sleigh....not a Sikorsky."

"What are you reading?" Riley asked Murphy.

"Just a little poem I wrote."

"What's it about?" asked Lamb, sitting down on an empty ammo crate.

"Christmas," answered Murphy seriously.

"Let's hear it," said Riley as some of the other members of the squad gathered around.

"Naw, I don't want to." Murphy started to fold the piece of paper up.

"Aw come on, man. We ain't gonna laugh," coaxed Lamb.

"Well, okay. Here goes..." Murphy cleared his throat.

"'Twas the night before Christmas,
  and all thru the bunker,
  I was on watch,
  and the rest were in slumber.
  But visions of sugar plums,
  don't dance in my head,
  I wear a steel pot,
  so I don't end up dead!
  But the night's not a waste,

we do have a goal,
they're taking my squad
out on patrol.
And we'll have us a party
when we get to the sticks,
if we can get by the sentry
at Gate Number Six.
We'll get us a tree,
and decorate it up,
with hand grenades and trip flares
and other fancy stuff.
But up in the air,
what's that I see?
Look's like St. Nick,
in a Huey one-B.
He's rolling in left,
he's rolling in hot,
Out in the open,
it looks like we're caught.
He fires a burst,
continues his attack,
I now see why mama-san
dyed my uniforms black!'"

Murphy looked around sheepishly and began folding the page. Lamb was the first to speak. "Is that it?"

"Yeah, what do ya think?"

"Sucks," said Lamb without a second's hesitation as he rose to leave.

"Merry fuckin' Christmas to you too!" called Murphy after him. Turning back to the others, he said, "That Lamb is full of shit."

Riley sat down on the hot sand next to Galleon. The poncho stretched overhead offered little respite from the heat, but the shade it provided was better than nothing. Monsoon season was almost over, and the rains came more seldom and with diminishing ferocity.

Mail had come in a welcome, but unusual way. Santa Claus had dropped into the base camp aboard a Sikorsky. His red-suited form could be seen for a half mile, leaning out the side door on the M-60 machine gun mount and waving to the troops as they made their approach into the landing zone. With a hearty "Ho-ho-ho" and a "Merry Christmas", Santa tossed out the mail bags, cases of c-rations and...ammo.

Lamb helped drag the supplies away from the helicopter and screamed over the sound of the roaring Pratt & Whitney at the white-bearded man in red, "HEY SANTA, WHAT'S THE MACHINE GUN FOR?"

Stevens looked at him, paused for a second and said, "For them that are naughty, not nice!"

"Whatcha got there?" asked Toby.

"Letter from Patty, and a package from home," answered Riley, tearing open the envelope.

"Open the package first, man," pleaded Galleon, envisioning Christmas cookies or pogey bait.

"Later man. First things first." Riley settled back against a wall of sandbags and began to read.

Dear Jeff,

I hope this finds you well and having a nice Christmas. I spoke with your mother, and she said she sent you a package for the holiday. I hope it arrives by Christmas day. I saw your brother on the beach yesterday, and noticed that he had your surfboard. He said it was
alright, and that he was just keeping it in "shape" for you. Ha!

Everything here is still about the same, but some of your friends are leaving and may not be here when you return. Jimmy Wright joined the AirForce, and wants to be a medic.

Lee Holt just came home for the holidays from college, and I found out he is in Naval ROTC. (Some of the kids say ROTC stands for "Run Off To Canada", Ha!)

Pete Jacobs has turned hippie, and is up in Berkeley. I heard he burned his draft card, but later found out it was only a photocopy. He never has been the brave sort.

Baby, I miss you! I worry every day about you, and am terrified every time I see the six o'clock news and they show scenes of Vietnam and the fighting. Every day I pray that you are safe, and I'm counting the days until you come home.Please take care of yourself, and write every chance you get. I LOVE YOU!!
I've got to go for now, but will write again in a couple of days. Until then,

All My Love, Kisses....
Patti

Riley's head settled back against the wall and he closed his eyes. His mind escaped the war and drifted to scenes of Patti, his glossy black Chevy Impala, and the nights of parking on the last row of the drive-in theater. He chuckled as he thought of his task of trying to catch enough of the movie to be able to tell his parents what it was about. His sexual antics with Patti held top priority on their Friday night dates, but his parents always asked questions about the plot of the film. He knew that this was their only way of checking up on him to make sure that he didn't get himself or Patti into trouble. They didn't like her anyway, and wished that he would date someone from his church instead. She was a Catholic. Riley could hear his mother's words, "Jeffrey, what you need is a good little Baptist girl...." Wonder what she would say if I brought home a good little Buddhist girl...

Riley carefully folded the letter and placed it back in it's envelope. He put the letter in a plastic bag with the others he had saved and stuck them in his shirt pocket for re-reading later.

The package was the one that the letter had mentioned, and yielded a small canned ham, some packages of popping corn and several kinds of candy bars, most of which had melted into a gooey brown mess in their wrappers. It also contained a home town newspaper and several recent magazines. On the cover of one was a large photo of a "Peace Demonstration". Several people Riley's age were in the process of marching down a street carrying a Vietcong flag.

"Toby, check this shit out!" said Riley, shoving the magazine at Galleon who was busy trying to separate a chocolate bar from its package.

"Where the hell did they get that?" he asked, not seeing the point.

"Who cares? The thing is, here we are trying to fight this war for Mom, apple pie and hot dogs and these pukes are runnin' around protesting us and carrying a VC flag. How in the hell do they get away with this shit?"

"Wonder if that's one of Williams' flags? Could be one that some Air Force zoomie took home," said Galleon, still wondering where they got it.

"Galleon, sometimes I think you are a definite lost cause."

The small group of replacements crossed the Rao Nai River west of Hue just after dark, when their detection would be less likely. Dharkov had seen the little round basket boats before, but this was the first time he had actually been in one. The boats were woven from reeds, stretched over a round frame and coated with a water-proofing material. Simple, but effective.   The river had been their last physical obstacle before the tunnel complex headquarters. He was almost there.

Chapter Sixteen

It was time. Truong entered Da Nang as he had before, and arrived at the old man's house as he had been directed. He was fearful that the one called

Diem may have betrayed him for profit, but his mission was more important than his safety.

Like clockwork, Diem appeared on schedule. He entered the small room at the rear of the house and seated his finely tailored body in the same wooden chair, lighting a cigarette. "I have good news for you, ha-si."

"Yes? And what might that news be?"

"I may have found the man of which you seek. It has been very difficult, and of course expensive, but I may be able to help you," said the South Vietnamese Captain.

"How expensive?" asked Truong warily.

"Not more than you can afford," smiled Diem. "What can you afford?"

"What can you tell me?" countered Truong.

"The yellow-haired one is named Riley. He also is a ha-si, in the American Marines. He was the leader of the ones who battled you at Khuong My, and was taken away by helicopter. The number of the machine that you provided me was quite helpful, and I personally have seen this man. I was there the day that he and his men were delivered to the air base. I even have copies of the reports that he and his squad gave to the American captain that I work with." Diem put a manila envelope on the table and smiled, exhaling a cloud of blue smoke.

"How expensive?" Truong repeated.

"What can you pay?" countered Diem.

"I have this," said Truong, placing a small handful of gold jewelry on the table. It included Uncle Quan's gold ring with the ruby stone setting. It had been in the family many years, and Truong hated parting with it, but this task was much more important than sentimental feelings.

"I am afraid that this is not enough." Diem pulled another puff from the cigarette held in the French manner between his thumb and forefinger. As he did so, he looked down at the small collection of jewelry with an expression of scorn. Truong knew he was trying to raise the price. Like most Vietnamese merchants, he always tried for a higher price. But Truong knew how to bargain.

"And I am afraid that that is all I have. Now, if you wish to leave with this reward, I ask that you provide me with further information. I need to know where to find this Riley."

"It is because I wish to help the cause that I provide you with your answer," said Diem feigning indignation. "The jewelry is only to cover expenses."

"Of course," said Truong, knowing that Diem had no expenses, and the information was easily obtained by one in the right place. And Diem obviously was in the right place.

"He is with his company. They are at this moment at a camp near An Hoa. The camp is located north of there and can be found quite easily. Look for a hill of sand with fortifications. On this hill is a temple shrine known as the 'Temple of the Five Dragons'. The local villagers know of this place." Diem snuffed out his cigarette, blew out the last lungful of smoke and picked up the gold. Standing, he turned to leave.

"You will be remembered for your help in this matter." Truong said as he stood. He watched

Diem leave and waited for ten minutes before he departed.

Yes, thought Truong, I will remember you well.

The American advisor to the Vietnamese soldiers could be easily seen in the Dragunov's scope.

Dharkov ignored the buzz of insects that persistently tried to distract him, and concentrated on the pointer-post and cross hatch wires of the scope as they played on his target. He had ranged the target in his scope's stadia line range finder and determined within a few meters exactly where the target was.

He would enjoy himself with this one. It had been too long, and he was going to take his time. His thumb curved through the open rear stock of the pistol grip, and the sensitive pre-set trigger fit his index finger perfectly. Now he would show the monkeys how it was done.

The ARVN patrol, first detected by the squad of communist soldiers--a squad Dharkov attached himself to when he found that they would be scouting near an ARVN outpost--stopped in plain view at the edge of a rice paddy. The nearest man turned around and motioned toward the American, who immediately came forward. Dharkov could see the Yankee, with his map in hand, make his way past the other patrol members until he came to the first man in the column. The range was only about four hundred meters. An easy shot. Dharkov decided to play with him, both to make a point to the observing North Vietnamese soldiers and to satisfy his own desires.

He waited until the American knelt next to the scout and watched him unfold his map. He shifted his aim to the man kneeling behind the American and settled the pointer on his throat. He estimated the bullet drop to cause the bullet to impact on his chest. A good heart shot. Dharkov also could see that his target carried binoculars. Maybe he was a leader. "Tell your men to hold their fire. I want them to observe this only," whispered Dharkov, without taking his eye from the scope. He eased the slack off the trigger and felt the resistance of the catch just before the sear released the hammer. The Dragunov bucked in recoil as the bullet discharged. Dharkov's practiced eye did not leave the scope. He kept his cheek glued to the stock and the rifle settled back on target. The ARVN soldier was not to be seen. He had apparently been knocked backwards into the brush behind his position. Dharkov shifted to the American. The Yankee had dropped to his stomach, as had the rest of the patrol, and was busily looking around in confusion.

Dharkov shifted to the point man. The lead man had also dropped to the prone position, and only raised up momentarily in an apparent act of seeking a route of escape. Dharkov knew that they would be confused and would not be able to tell where the shot originated from. He let the SVD settle on the man's position and waited.

In less than a minute the point looked up again, and his head was transformed into a cloud of pink mist. The American clearly did not know what to do next, but took the initiative and began yelling orders to the troops behind him. They could not hear him, or paid little attention, for they were too busy firing across the paddies in confusion. The ARVNs did not let a lack of visible targets prevent them from making noise and shooting up the landscape in a desperate act of defense.

Now Dharkov settled on the American. He took his time. The American was busy trying to bring order to the confusion caused by Dharkov's first two shots, and his bravery was exhibited by his lack of concern for his own safety. Dharkov fired.

The first shot hit the Yankee advisor in his right thigh, crippling him. He spun from his crouched position and lay on his back, rolling in pain. Dharkov watched as an ARVN tried to make his way to the American, and stopped his progress with a shot to the head. The observing NVA soldiers chattered in amazement as they watched the little man's helmet turn end-over-end in the air before disappearing in the brush. Dharkov breathed for relaxation and again drew a bead.

The American had pulled himself up to his hands and knees, trailing his wounded leg, grotesquely twisted behind him, and tried to crawl down the trail to cover. Dharkov took aim again, squeezed the trigger, and shot the remaining good leg. Now the NVA were indeed chattering like monkeys and pointing in amusement.

Dharkov could barely see the Yankee now. He lay on his back, his upper torso obviously convulsed in pain. Occasionally an arm would raise into the air, warning the others to stay away, but each time it appeared a bit more feeble. Dharkov let the Dragunov fall to rest on the green-shirted form. He fired again and saw a puff of dust fly from the victim's chest. He knew it was a hit, but not a solid strike. He needed a little more target.

Another ARVN, bravely ignoring the American's warning, tried to run to the wounded man to drag him out of the line of fire. Dharkov stopped him ten meters short with a single shot. That was easy, thought Dharkov. Are there any more of you as foolish as that one?

The American tried to roll away, and as a last act of defiance, used his remaining good arm to drag his pistol from his holster. What do you think you are going to do with that? Dharkov aimed once more and ended the act of defiance with a head shot. It was time to break contact. If the ARVNs were the slightest bit competent, they would already be on the radio asking for help, artillery, or worse-- air cover. Dharkov had already violated his own rules of engagement by firing more than three shots before changing positions, but he was confident in the inability of the South Vietnamese soldiers to counter his threat. He would not try the same thing with an experienced group of Americans. He motioned the NVA soldiers to silence as he led the way back into the shadows of bamboo.

Yes, these hairless apes do indeed sound like chattering monkeys.

Chapter Seventeen

Christmas passed with little to mark it as a holiday occasion. There was no snow, no shoppers, no decorations and no visible change in the local population. The Christmas carols on AFRS radio only served to remind the men in the field what they were missing. New Years was little different, but at least the platoon had access to bottles of "45", a local imitation of whiskey, and celebrated New Years Eve with a small party. Lamb had provided cheese and crackers that he had hoarded from several cases of C-rations, and at midnight the company opened up the "FPL", or Final Protective Line with all weapons firing for one minute. Artillery provided star-cluster and parachute flares, and the display ended with Riley's squad singing what they could remember of Auld Lang Syne.

Two days later, a formation was called. The fact of a formation in the field was very unusual, and those not on watch attended apprehensively. They fully expected the VC to hit them with incoming mortar rounds, or at least sniper fire, as soon as they lined up.

"Companeee....aaatennn...SHUN!" yelled the Gunny. The company snapped to for the first time in months, and the gunnery sergeant did a smart about face and saluted the captain. "Sir, the company is formed."

The Gunny then took three steps to the side of the Skipper and did a smart about face, facing the company, who still wondered what the dog-and-pony-show was all about. The Gunny took a small stack of papers from the Captain and began to read;

"Know all men by these presents, greetings. The Commandant of the Marine Corps, having bestowed special trust and confidence in the below named individuals hereby promotes them to the rank of Sergeant, United States Marine Corps, and to rank as such until relieved by proper authority." In alphabetical order, the Captain read the names; "Anderson, Baker, Cunningham," went the list. It was about time the "Crotch" had provided promotions. They were long overdue. "...Jackson, Langford, Riley..."

Riley felt his tensed body relax. He had expected it, but still couldn't believe it. He damned sure could use the extra pay, and his dad would be proud of his new rank, but most of all, he really started to feel like a squad leader. Sergeant Riley, he said to himself. Has a nice ring to it...

The Gunny read another list of names for corporal, and then a list for lance corporal. Galleon made lance, and Lamb elbowed him with a grin. "Well, Lance, betcha never thought a Colorado beaner like you would ever make it. Neither did we!" snickered Lamb.

"You forget one thing, oh faithless one..." Galleon elbowed Lamb back.

"Oh, and what's that?"

"I know someone big!"

"Bullshit. Who?"

"I know Sergeant Riley," replied Galleon seriously.

"So fuckin' what?" asked Lamb, wanting Galleon to get to the point.

"He is an old surfin' buddy of the Commandant."

"Man, cut me some slack," whispered Lamb.

"The fact remains, private, that I am now a Lance Corporal, and Riley is a Sergeant, and you are still a PFC. So, square your ass away, unfuck your attitude, and be a good little Private and maybe, just maybe, I'll mention you to my friend Sergeant Riley, and he'll talk to his friend the Commandant and we can get you promoted."

"Don't do me any fuckin' favors."

Just then the first mortar round sailed into the perimeter and the formation came to an early close with the Marines' rapid return to their sandy holes.

Truong once again saw Marble Mountain, and wondered how the old rock ape, Ho, was doing. He continued south, past the Cau Do River, and entered the sandy terrain of the coastal plains northwest of Hoi An. He too judged the area excellent terrain for sniper activities, and thanked Buddha for providing Riley to him in such a way. Now all he had to do was find the American's camp and wait.

The young Vietcong thought of his thieu-'uy and wondered how angry he would be by now. He had not reported back since his meeting with Diem. Perhaps the lieutenant thought him dead. It was indeed possible, and if this was the case, he would now be a hero. Many of Truong's friends had become heroes.

Darkness came as Truong approached the old railroad bridge across the Ky Lam river. He knew he had to cross the river, and did not know if the bridge was in the hands of the imperialists or not. After ascertaining that it was void of human presence, he made his way cautiously across. He was ready to leap into the river if he was challenged or detected by an enemy on the opposite bank. There was no one. This river was his last physical obstacle, and Truong also took this bit of luck as a sign from Buddha.

He had traveled a long way and the Dragunov weighed heavy in his arms. It was time to rest. Truong found a tiny abandoned shrine in a small village, crawled in and curled up. He would wait until morning and then ask the village chief where the Temple of Five Dragons could be found. Once he gained this information, he would find Riley. Since Truong now knew the yellow-haired one's name, he thought of it often. It burned in his mind.

Dharkov listened as the North Vietnamese colonel went over the plan for attack that he had just received. It was simple, but it was daring. The key element was surprise. They would attack in several places at once. Saigon itself would be infiltrated and hit by many small groups of guerrillas. The same would happen in most major cities and many provincial capitals. Dharkov also knew that the Marine base at Khe Sanh would be surrounded and attacked by both troops and artillery that had been secretly emplaced in the surrounding hills. Another Dien Bien Phu, thought Dharkov with a smile. The Capitalists never learn.

Dharkov thought back to his military history classes and remembered the battle between the French and the Vietminh at Dien Bien Phu. The French had built a complex of fortified posts in the Plain of Jars in the western sector of what is now North Vietnam. They were surrounded by Ho Chi Minh's Vietminh troops who had dragged artillery into the surrounding mountains, much like Khe Sanh. The only difference was the French positions were in an area of low ground, and the Vietminh held the hills. After two bloody months, the final French positions fell, and with it the airstrip. Over six thousand French and colonial troops, low on supplies and ammunition, surrendered. The Americans would be lucky if any were allowed to surrender.

Dharkov broke his daydreaming to listen to the rest of the plan for the action at Hue. Two battalions of the 6th North Vietnamese Army Regiment would attack from the southwest along the Huong River and press straight for the ARVN headquarters in the city. One battalion would secure the road and the railroad north of the city, and the 4th Regiment would attack from the south and take the American Military Advisor compound. They would be assisted by six Vietcong battalions. It was a simple matter of overwhelming the defenders, and it was to be a total surprise. Dharkov hoped that the simultaneous attacks on the other cities would cause so much confusion that aid could not be sent to the enemy.

Foremost in Dharkov's mind was his role. As an observer, he gained permission to move about at will. This would serve his purposes perfectly. He wished he was in a command position, but then he was not particularly interested in leading these monkeys into combat. What I wouldn't do for a battalion of Russian airborne troops, thought the Major.

The final element that would aid the plan was the planned cease fire that would accompany the TET New Year. Many things would work in their favor.

"GOOD MORNIN-G-G-G-G   VIET..NA-M-M-M-M...."

Galleon turned up the transistor radio and settled back against the sandbag wall to listen to the only radio station that would play the music that reminded him of home.

"This is your link with reality, your spinner of disks and your master of the platter, Specialist 'Vinnie-the-Voice' Barnett, coming at you live from Armed Forces Radio, Saigon. Before we hit you with the latest and greatest from the States, we have a few updates you'll be glad to hear. So for you grunts out there in the field, and you sailors out there on the deep blue...here's your favorite lady with the news. Take it awayyy...SHELLEY.

Riley, Lamb and Karlov gathered around to listen.

"I'm sure glad this ain't TV," said Lamb sitting down.

"Why's that, man?" asked Karlov taking his helmet off.

"'Cause she's probably a pig, man."

"Why do you say that?" asked Galleon, expecting a set-up.

"Anybody with a sexy voice like that that comes to Vietnam where there's a million horny dudes gotta be a pig. Otherwise, she'd get a job at home." Lamb jammed a couple of pieces of c-ration gum in his mouth.

"Maybe she's just patriotic," Riley shot back. Sometimes Lamb really got on his nerves.

"Okay, so she's a patriotic pig."

"For all you handsome guys from I Corps to the Delta, this should cheer you up. The government of North Vietnam proposed that peace talks commence and the United States Government, in a show of good faith, agreed to cease bombing in the vicinity of Hanoi in observance of the TET Lunar New Year...."

The news continued with optimistic reporting of events that were currently taking place that may signal the end of the war.

"How about that shit?" said Lamb excitedly. "I bet we get outta here before rotation date!"

"If you believe that crap, I got an opium mine to sell you." Galleon sniffed in disgust and picked up his M40. He checked the action, dusted off the lenses and replaced the plastic caps. "I don't know about you guys, but I think the Commies have something up their sleeve."

"I dunno," said Karlov. "It has been kind of quiet for a few days."

Riley brushed a mosquito away and looked at Karlov. "The calm before the storm, man. The calm before the storm."

Chapter Eighteen

The two American prisoners stood under the mango tree with their hands bound behind their backs. Dharkov had been summoned for the interrogation since he spoke English fluently, as did many Russians. He noted that the two prisoners had been stripped of their shirts and stood barefoot as a security measure to hamper any attempt at escape.

The NVA interrogator had not been able to glean much information from the two enlisted soldiers, and was becoming frustrated at their answers to his questions. He could not tell if they did not know the answers, or simply refused to cooperate.

Dharkov picked up one of the green nylon jungle shirts that lay at the feet of one of the prisoners and examined it. He noted the shoulder patch, recognized it as the shield and sword of MACV and made a mental note. He also saw the subdued embroidered tape over the left breast pocket with the words "U S ARMY". Over the right pocket was the name tag--"CARSON". The collars denoted the three stripes and rocker of Staff Sergeant.

"Allow me to assist," Dharkov said to the North Vietnamese officer.

"Very well, comrade Major. It seems that they are either stupid or fail to see their predicament." The North Vietnamese stepped back.

Shifting to English, Dharkov looked at the American whose shirt he held. "Sergeant Carson, I am going to ask you a few questions. Many of the answers I already know, so if I see that you try to lie to me it will go badly for you and your friend."

Carson looked at Dharkov. The strange looking Oriental appeared calm and in control of the situation. He wore no rank insignia, yet the other gooks stepped back to let him take over.

Dharkov continued. "Sergeant, there is no reason to withhold information from us. There is no escape, and your cooperation will dictate the kind of treatment you will receive. Now I am going to ask you some very simple questions. First, what is the name of your unit?"

"The United States Army," replied Carson, knowing that according to the Geneva Convention, he was only required to give name, rank and serial number. He knew that it was obvious he was in the army.

"I know that, Sergeant. I feel that you underestimate us. I ask you once more, what is your unit?"

"Carson, Frederick B., Staff Sergeant, RA4357768."

Dharkov hit the American in the stomach with such force that it doubled him over gasping for breath. "You are with the Military Advisory

Command. Failure to answer correctly will only cause you and your comrade great pain. Now, how many Americans are in Hue?"

Carson tried to straighten up.   "Carson, Fred..."

Dharkov slapped him across the face, bringing blood to his mouth.   "Where is your headquarters?" Dharkov knew the answer to this one already. The MACV headquarters was in the southeast sector of Hue. That was not secret.

"Carson..."

Dharkov planted his boot on the bare foot of the soldier and ground his heel as he watched the Americans eyes for an indication of pain. "You are not cooperating.   You must realize that your comrades in Hue already think you dead. As far as they are concerned, you no longer exist. We can do anything we want to you. I do not wish to harm you, but I too, have a mission."

Screw your mission, thought Carson. And screw you, you Commie puke! "Carson, Fred...." Again Dharkov hit him.

"I weary of this one. Perhaps it is time to make a point." Dharkov took his Tokarev pistol from his holster and worked the slide. He placed it between Carson's eyes. "Now, my friend, you have exactly ten seconds to tell me how many American pigs are in Hue."

Carson closed his eyes and his mind was flooded with a kaleidoscope of thoughts. Home, his girl, his car, Mom.....

Dharkov now watched the second Americans face with his peripheral vision as he squeezed the trigger.

CLICK!

Carson exhaled in both relief and terror. His fellow prisoner, PFC Jenkins, began to shake.

"Ahhhh, it seems that the empty chamber has given you another chance. Perhaps you now see what may happen?"

Carson did have a change of attitude, but not what Dharkov expected. Carson's face changed from one of fear to one of hatred. He spat at Dharkov. He was rewarded by a knee to his groin, which collapsed him to the ground.

"Insolent pig!" spat the Russian. "I will show you what happens to one such as you!" Dharkov grabbed Carson under the arm and jerked him to his feet. With no show of emotion, he dragged him out of sight into a grove of banana trees and tied him to one. After he was satisfied that the American was immobilized, he tore a strip of cloth from the jungle shirt and rolled it into a ball. This he jammed into Carson's mouth. He then tore another strip and wrapped it around the Americans head, effectively gagging him. This done, he pulled a loaded magazine from a pouch on his belt and inserted it into the Tokarev with a distinct "click". "Now, foolish one, you will see what Russian ingenuity will do!"

The word "Russian" struck Carson's mind like a hot poker.

Dharkov aimed his pistol in the air and fired a shot. He then turned with a smirk and walked back to the first prisoner.

Approaching him alone, he let Jenkins see the smoking pistol. "Now, young one, you see what the reward is for insolence. I give you the chance to live. How many Americans are in Hue?"

By now, the PFC was terrified. He knew that even if he cooperated, he would still be killed. "I don't know," he replied, shaking.

"That is not the correct answer. I will give you one more chance. I realize that as a private, you are not privy to a great deal of useful information, but there are some things I feel you may know that will aid us in our struggle. Do you not wish to see the war end?"

"Of course, but I really don't know anything..."

Dharkov cut him short. "You know how many men are in your unit, don't you?"

"If I tell you that, I'll be a traitor."

"Is it not better to be a traitor, than to be dead? When the war is over, no one will even know that you cooperated with us and you will be released to return home. Do you not wish to go home?"

"I wish I never came here to begin with," said Jenkins truthfully. Dharkov began to feel he was making progress. Now if he could just keep him talking.

"Do you have a wife or a girlfriend at home?" asked Dharkov pulling a pack of cigarettes from his pocket.

"I'm not married," said the the soldier. He was only eighteen.

"Do you not wish to have a family someday?"

"Of course."

"That will be very hard to do if I discharge this pistol into your manhood," said Dharkov matter-of-factly, lighting his cigarette.

Jenkins mind immediately flashed to his imagined fate of Sergeant Carson. "Please sir, I really don't know anything."

"You do know many things. You just don't realize you know them. Perhaps I can help you remember." Dharkov placed the muzzle of the nine millimeter pistol against Jenkins crotch. "How many men are in your unit?"

Jenkins looked down, then up to the Major's face. Dharkov's expression was impassive. Jenkins was convinced he would pull the trigger. "Twelve." he said in barely a whisper.

"What? Louder!"

"Twelve!"

"Good.   See? You really did know something.   Now, What is your commanding officer's name?"

After thirty minutes of questioning, Dharkov was convinced Jenkins could provide no more useful information. He left the shade of the mango tree and went back to Carson. After cutting his bonds, he dragged the bloody American back to his comrade. Jenkins was at first relieved to find Carson still alive, then angry with himself for cooperating with the Russian.

Dharkov removed the gag from Carson's mouth and again stood him next to Jenkins. "Your comrade has been extremely helpful. He has saved your life. Now, let us see if you can save his."

The Russian holstered the pistol and took an AK-47 from one of the Vietnamese guards, unfolding the spike bayonet, he snapped it into place. He then pushed Jenkins backwards until his back was against the trunk of the mango tree. Dharkov raised the Kalashnikov and pressed the bayonet against Jenkins bare chest, just below the left shoulder.

"Sergeant Carson, how many men are in your unit?"

Carson had seen how the Russian could bluff, and if Jenkins had cooperated, surely he would not be hurt.

"Go piss up a rope."

A look of amusement crossed Dharkov's face as he imagined the suggested act. "I do not see what that would accomplish." Dharkov then leaned against the AK and forced the pointed tip of the bayonet slightly through Jenkins skin and into the pectoral muscle. Jenkins screamed with pain as blood began to trickle from the small triangular wound.

"Perhaps now you will reconsider?"

"CUT ME LOOSE AND LET'S SEE HOW BRAVE YOU ARE, YOU SON OF A BITCH!"

"You would like that, wouldn't you?" smiled Dharkov without raising his voice. He then placed the bayonet against Jenkins other shoulder. "How many men?"

"CARSON, FREDERICK..."

Dharkov drove the bayonet through Jenkins shoulder, pinning him to the tree. With a twist, he extracted it allowing Jenkins to fall to the ground.

"I will allow you another opportunity. How many men?"

"Three, you bastard. Three!"

"I do not feel you are being truthful with me." Dharkov immediately raised the AK to Jenkins right knee and pulled the trigger. The kneecap shattered and the joint disintegrated as blood erupted from the wound in a small red burst. Jenkins passed out from the pain.

"You're just gonna kill us anyway!" screamed Carson with a face crimson with rage. Jenkins was only a jeep driver, and had only been in Vietnam for two months. He was just a kid. Carson had had all this he could stand. He doubled over and charged Dharkov, catching the Russian by surprise before his captors could react. Dharkov had not been prepared, and was knocked to the ground. Carson immediately raised his bare foot and drove it into the side of Dharkov's head. The Major saw a flash of light as the pain of the kick shot through his head. The guards finally reacted and grabbed Carson by the hair. One of them raised his bound hands above his shoulders causing him to bend forward from the waist. Another drove his knee into Carson's face. Dharkov, in a rage, regained his feet.

"A brave but futile act. I weary of this." The Russian slid the safety off on the AK and pointed it at Jenkins head.

Krack!

Jenkins would never go home.

"I give you one more chance to save your life," said Dharkov, his head still reeling in pain from Carson's kick. He aimed the rifle at the center of Carson's face.

Carson stared first at the smoking muzzle of the weapon, then at Dharkov. The Russian was losing face with the Vietnamese captors. They in turn found his actions amusing. They had encountered the will of American prisoners before. It was obvious that he had not.

"Damn you! How many?" Dharkov acted as if he was beginning to lose control.

Carson closed his eyes. Dharkov waited almost ten seconds before lowering the weapon. He looked at Carson and smiled. He could not deprive the Vietnamese of a possible intelligence source. Carson obviously had knowledge that could prove useful, but Dharkov chose not to pursue it at this time.

Dharkov looked at the circle of Vietnamese. "When this one is weakened with hunger and lack of sleep, he will surely prove more cooperative." Having saved face, he handed the weapon to a guard and walked away.

For many days, the Vietcong and North Vietnamese, wearing civilian clothes and impersonating students, businessmen and off-duty South Vietnamese soldiers, infiltrated the cities of the South. They were now in position and awaited the beginning of the offensive. North Vietnam had taken advantage of the holiday cease-fire, and moved their celebration up one day. They would celebrate on the eve of TET. The sole purpose was to free the holiday itself for the surprise attack. It was to catch the South at its weakest time. Many ARVN soldiers would be on leave to visit families, and others were expected to relax in a false sense of security due to the peace talks and cease fire.

A few ARVN generals feared that something was up, and denied leave to their men. This affected one division in Saigon, and two more in other parts of country. The Americans by now had also determined that something was amiss, and prepared themselves for the worst. History would show that these actions by the American command structure, and the intuition of a few South Vietnamese generals, would turn a probable disaster into a victory.

Chapter Nineteen

Truong awoke before the sun came up and crept to the door of the small bare temple-shrine. It was a one room affair, with a six-foot ancient crudely made Buddha sitting cross-legged on a concrete pedestal against one wall. In its clasped hands, a small pot of dirt rested to hold burning incense sticks. Truong noted the small red sticks stuck in the dirt, now burned down stubs that gave evidence of many past prayers. The temple was old, but obviously not abandoned. He now would try to find the village chief or an elder who could answer his questions.

He walked to the side of the open doorway and listened cautiously for any non-Vietnamese voices. After a few minutes of hearing only the sing-song of familiar chatter emanating from the grass huts, he left the temple and walked down the central trail of the village.

After walking only fifty meters, he came across a stoop shouldered old man with a whispy white goatee carrying a hoe. Wearing the traditional conical sun hat, white long-sleeve shirt and loose black pants, it was obvious to Truong that he was heading for the rice paddies for a day's toil. Truong stepped out onto the center of the path from the bushes. "Chao ong, Grandfather,"

The old man stopped at the salutation and examined the greeter. He noted the scoped rifle, the canvas belt, suspenders and the magazine pouches and grenades embracing Truong's body. His face was impassive, but he was apprehensive. He had seen too much war, and this could only mean that the war was once again manifesting itself on his quiet village.

"Chao ong, young soldier. Why are you here?"

"I seek only directions, sir. Are you the Chief of this village?" asked Truong, showing great respect. He had come from a village much like this one, and had always been taught to respect the elders. He also knew that it would gain him more information in return.

The elder was somewhat impressed, but still cautious. He had seen what the Vietcong could do to make a point. His own niece had been executed in front of the entire village as an example of the futility of resistance to the National Liberation Front. Her crime was being the wife of a district police officer.

"I am not the chief, but I may be able to help you with directions if that is all you want. What directions do you seek?" He only wanted to see the Vietcong leave them in peace.

"I wish to know the location of a temple known as the 'Temple of Five Dragons'. I understand it is not far."

"You are alone?" asked the old one looking around.

"Yes. I only seek the temple to honor a wish from my family that I visit it like my father, and his father had. I wish to say a prayer for them," Truong lied.

"I see. I am afraid that it is impossible for you to go there at this time. Perhaps you would return some other day?"

"Why can I not go there now?" asked Truong, his hopes rising.

"The temple is old and unused. It has become part of an American military camp. I am afraid they may not welcome one such as you," smiled the elder.

"I see. Perhaps you are right. If I can find a way to return in the future, where shall I go?"

"The 'Temple of Five Dragons' is just over four kilometers in that direction." The old man pointed to the southeast. "It is located at the base of a large hill of sand. You will see the hill before you see the temple."

"Cam on ong, Grandfather." Truong thanked him.

"Khong co gi, young man." You are welcome, said the elder. He shouldered his hoe and continued on his way.

Four kilometers, thought Truong as he set off down the path. I will travel three kilometers and two hundred meters, Uncle Quan will travel the last eight-hundred meters to Riley.

After an all night patrol, the squad tried to rest as much as possible in the shade of their poncho hooches. This was almost impossible in the shimmering heat. It was over a hundred and twenty degrees fahrenheit, and even though most of the Marines had been in Vietnam for ten months, they still found it difficult to sleep during the day. Only utter exhaustion could accomplish that task.

By noon Riley could sleep no more. The heat had become like a blast furnace, reflecting from the dirty-white sand in undulating waves. He re-read some of his letters from Patty, and promised himself that he would write one to her later. He opened his willy-peter bag on his packboard and extracted his book of Kipling's Prose and Verse. It was ironic that he opened it to the page of a poem titled "Tommy Atkins". He couldn't help but remember the article he had read about the "peace" march in the magazine his family sent him, and remembered some of the things these "hippies" said about "murderers, baby killers, and hooch burners. "Baby killers...where do they get that shit?" thought Riley as he tried to concentrate on his reading....

        "...Yes, makin' mock of uniforms that guard you while you sleep,

Is cheaper than them uniforms, an' they're starvation cheap;

An' hustlin' drunken soldiers when they're goin' large a bit,

Is five times better business than paradin' in full kit.

        Riley closed his eyes and imagined the British soldier in India in the late 1800's. He felt better knowing that his generation was not the first to encounter civilian hostility. He read on.

Then it's Tommy this, an' Tommy that, an' "Tommy,'ow's yer soul?"

But it's "Thin red line of 'eroes" when the drums begin to roll--

The drums begin to roll, my boy's, the drums begin to roll,

O it's "Thin red line of 'eroes" when the drums begin to roll.

Riley finished the poem, then turned to his favorite--"Gunga Din". He marveled at the Indian water boy's similarity to some of the South Vietnamese irregulars he had worked with.

"Hey Riley....er, Sergeant Riley, what ya readin'?" asked Lamb walking up.

"Rudyard Kipling."

"Who?"

"You've never heard of Kipling?" asked Riley as he closed the book.

"Nah, who was he?"

"He was a story writer. He also wrote a lot of poems about the British Army in India during Queen Victoria's time."

"Queen who?" asked Lamb with little apparent interest.

"Never mind."

As the old man had said, Truong saw the sand hill before he saw the temple. He had been traveling cautiously for the past kilometer, and now kept only to the cover of the small evergreen trees. He moved from one tree to the next, carefully scanning the surrounding terrain before he did so. Like most American camps, the area around the hill had been cleared of brush and trees for almost five hundred meters. This afforded the camp's defenders a good visual range of the surrounding area, and offered little cover to an approaching enemy. It also afforded an enemy sniper, such as Truong, excellent fields of fire. Again Buddha had smiled.

Truong hid in a small grove of pines and waited until the sun dropped below the western horizon. He overcame his urge to look for Riley first. That would wait. Major Dharkov had taught him well, and the first virtue of a sniper was patience. After dark, he chose his position for the next day and quietly scraped out a small hole in the sand. This took almost three hours, and he interrupted his excavation each time he thought he heard something. He knew the Marines sent out many patrols at night. As a small boy, Uncle Quan had told many stories of the war with the French. They did not go out of their forts at night unless they had to. The night belonged to the Vietminh. Now, the night was shared with the determined Americans.

When he was satisfied with his position, he moved almost a hundred meters away and carefully broke small branches from the short trees. He was careful not to take more than a few from any one tree, and when he had collected enough, he returned to the hole. By two-o'clock in the morning, he had woven a platform large enough to cover the hole. He left the green needles on the branches and laid it over the hole. Now he backed off and looked back at the position to check the camouflaged cover. It was good. He would only need it for one day, and was not worried about the foliage dying and changing color. If he did not accomplish his mission tomorrow, then he would move anyway. It was possible Riley was on the other side of the Imperialist perimeter, out of sight. He would know when the sun rose. Truong crawled into the hole and pulled the lid closed. It was time to wait.

"Gunny, did you put the word out to the men on that message we got from Regiment?" The captain was checking his small notebook to make sure he covered all his notes for the day, and found one several pages back that he had not crossed off.

"Which message was that, Skipper?"

"The one we got before Christmas about that gook sniper that has been raising hell along the perimeter."

"I mentioned it to the platoon sergeants, but since all them occurrences were up north, I didn't worry too much about it," replied the gunnery sergeant, sitting across the command bunker sharpening his K-bar.

"Yeah, well I want to make sure that we don't disregard any sniper fire if we get any. I know the men have been somewhat lax about it in the past, and it just may be that the gooks are learning how to shoot."

"That intel captain back at Regiment thinks this is just one slope, and if it is, the probability of him getting this far south ain't great."

The captain folded his notebook and stuck it in his pocket. "Gunny...just put the goddamned word out again, okay?"

"Aye-aye, sir."

Riley had to go on watch at 0400 hours, relieving Galleon who would get two more hours sleep before the sun came up. The new sergeant decided to call it a night and extinguished his red-lensed flashlight that he had been using to read under the cover of a poncho. He closed the book, placed it carefully back in the waterproof willy-peter bag, and lay down in the bottom of his fighting hole. As he drifted off to sleep, a line from one of Kipling's poems lingered hauntingly in his mind....

"There is a rock to the left, and a rock to the right, and low lean thorn between,
And ye may hear a breech-bolt snick where never a man is seen...."

Chapter Twenty

When the sun turned night into day once again, Riley built a make-shift desk from a c-ration box bridging two water cans. He smoothed out a piece of writing paper and began:

26 January, 1968
Somewhere in Vietnam.

Dear Patti,
Hi baby, it's me, down here at the war. I got your last letter, and the package from Mom. I shared the "pogey bait" with the guys in my squad and all-in-all, it wasn't a bad Xmas.

I just got promoted to sergeant, so will be able to send Mom more money. She has been banking it for me (US!), and it will come in handy later. There isn't anything to spend it on here anyway.

Don't worry about me, I'm fine other than the fact that I have lost about forty pounds since I got here. Most of that is probably due to dysentary, as we all have it. The standard joke is "you become Vietnam Qualified when you can shit through a keyhole at fifty meters". HA.

I've told you about the guys in my squad. You remember Lamb? He spends all his time trying to figure out a way to make money over here. Some of his ideas are really bizarre. Sometimes I think he is serious, though. I'll tell you about his ideas when I get home.

We thought we had some more action yesterday.

It sounded like we were being hit by all the VC in the world! It turned out to be nothing more than firecrackers! The Vietnamese have an annual celebration that they call TET. I don't know what that means, but they get real excited about it. It is their New Year celebration, and they all pop fireworks, party, and etc. If those firecrackers had gone off six months ago, we would have probably shot up the entire landscape and called in air strikes! But now we have a lot more fire discipline than we did then. Just think, I'm getting short! Just 63 days and a "wake-up"! Then I'll be on the big Silver Bird on my way back to you. I still haven't decided if I'm going to stay in the Corps or not. We'll talk about that later. Well, I got to go for now, so...

All my love,
Jeff

He folded the letter, put it in an envelope and wrote "FREE" where the stamp would normally go. Free postage was one of the few benefits one had in Vietnam. Here goes another "FPO" thought Riley as he addressed it. "FPO" stood for Fleet Post Office and was the designator for return addresses for Marines and sailors.

FPO San Francisco, thought Riley, Jesus. I wish I was there.

Foster plopped down next to Riley. "Sergeant Hays wants all the squad leaders up at the CP, mo-skoshe."

Riley looked up while licking the envelope flap. "Know what he wants?"

"No man, they don't tell me nothin'. After all, I don't surf with the Commandant," goaded Foster.

"Foster, in your case, I don't think even that would help you. You and your buddy Lamb are lost causes."

"Hey Sergeant, I can't even swim, much less surf," continued the small muscular black.

"Yeah? Well you better learn how. If anything happens to Peewee, you're the next tunnel rat."

"What the hell does swimming have to do with tunnels?" Foster's mind had not yet clicked to Riley's set-up.

"Just ask Peewee about tunnels, rivers and snakes." Riley stood to leave for the Command Post.

"Snakes? snakes? What choo mean, man? Dis Marine don't do no snakes!"

Truong elevated the camouflaged top that covered his hole six inches and peered out at the Marine

positions at the base of the hill. He could plainly
see the coiled concertina wire stacked one row on
two, the green tin cans containing small stones
hanging from the wire as make-shift rattles, and the
bunkers that stood plainly in view. Several Marines
were moving about, evidently not concerned with
danger. That was good.

The   Vietcong   marksman   eased   the
Dragunov up and drew the scope to his eye. He
slowly scanned the enemy emplacements looking
for his quarry. He would not give his presence
away by firing on anyone but the one called Riley.
He would take whatever time he needed for this.
Sooner or later, Buddha would smile again, and
Uncle Quan would speak.

"Good afternoon, Sergeant Riley," said Hays
sarcastically. "Glad to see you could make it. Are
you always the last lady to get the word?"

"I got here as soon as I found out that you
had a "Squad Leaders Up," answered Jeff, seating
himself just inside the door of the little temple. He
noted the other squad leaders were already there.

"Alright, listen up. I'll pass this intel sit-rep
around and I want you all to read it. It's about a
month old now, but the gunny wants everyone to be
aware of it. When we finish here, go back and brief
all your troops. It has to do with some gook sniper
that's supposed to be extremely accurate. My guess
is that he ain't no Cong. He's probably either a
Chink or maybe an Ivan. Back when this report
came out, the incidents were up north of Da Nang
just south west of the Hai Van. From there this

dude made his way slowly south around the edge of the enclave and the last hit was just east of Mieu Dong. Anyway, he ain't been heard from since, so maybe one of our patrols got him in an ambush, or he has moved to someplace else."

"Do they think it's just one dink?" asked Deitman, the third squad leader.

"Hell, who knows. Anyway, tighten up your people. There's two reasons: one, the sniper or snipers; and two, TET. We don't know what is gonna happen, but I'll tell you this: I don't trust no goddamned cease-fire. The friggin' Commies would rather tell a lie when the truth would help them, so watch your asses. Any questions?" Hays wiped sweat from his forehead with a green rag and looked around at the young faces.

"No? Well what are you waitin' for? Get outta my face!"

Truong could not help his reaction to the massive jolt of adrenalin that hit him when he saw his prey.
RILEY!
Truong tried to relax and remember everything he had been taught and experienced. This was no time for failure. He let the scope settle on the form of the man with yellow hair. Raising the scope to allow Riley's form to fill the range-finding stadia lines, he could see that the range was almost exactly six-hundred meters.

Do not rush, Dharkov's words sounded in his mind. Take your time and THINK! Plan each shot as if it were your only bullet! He followed the

American as he walked slowly across his field of vision toward a bunker behind the spiked wire.

Riley stopped by a fifty-five gallon drum that had a red-painted ammo box sitting on top of it. Truong could see him pull something small and white from his pocket, look at it momentarily, then raise the lid of the red box. He was standing still. Now was the time!

Riley took one last look at the letter. Then he bent forward to kiss it goodbye. At that precise micro-second, the 7.62 millimeter bullet destined for his brain grazed the short blond hair on the back of his head. The resounding crack of the bullet passing through the "sound barrier" as it went by reverberated in his ears. After the initial shock, Riley threw himself on the ground and crawled behind the steel drum for protection.

Truong cursed at Riley's luck and drew a bead on the barrel. Riley would have to come out. There was no other cover near, and Truong would wait.

"What the hell was that?" yelled a voice from the CP.

"Incoming!" rang Karlov's voice from his position.

"Sniper in the trees. Can't tell where," followed another.

Riley's only defense was his pistol. Once again he cursed both it and the Corps. "Galleon," he yelled.

"Yeah, man?"

"If that shitbag shoots again, try and see where it came from. Use your scope!" ordered Riley. He saw the letter to Patty laying on the ground not five meters away, where it fell. Gotta remember to make sure it gets in the mail....

Come to Uncle Quan, Riley. It is your time, thought Truong as he continued his sight-picture on the oil drum.

With no other incoming shots, Riley began to think the sniper may have left. He waited five more minutes while Toby scanned the little green pine trees. Nothing.

Riley decided to make a dash to his bunker and safety. "Toby, cover me. I'm comin' in!"

"Go man!"

Just as Riley took off in a crouch, another shot rang out and hit Riley's canteen. The impact of the high velocity bullet caused it to explode, knocking Riley off balance and spinning him to the ground. He scrambled in a low crawl as fast as he could toward Galleon. Toby still panned the terrain to his front, but could not tell where the second shot came from. Damn! this guy is good, thought Galleon. He knew he was up against an expert. Just let me see a fuckin' muzzle flash...just ONE!

Marine Riley, you are indeed a lucky one this day, thought Truong. He once again placed the sight on the scrambling form and eased back on the trigger.

Galleon's scan passed something odd. He had not noted it at first, but shifted back to check it out. It appeared to be a dark spot below a clump of pine needles.   What had caught his eye was an instantaneous flash of light of the sun reflecting off the lens of Truong's scope. There it is again!

Toby laid his forearm stock across the sand bags to steady his aim and squeezed off a shot. Sand kicked up where the thirty caliber bullet struck just outside Truong's hole. Truong ducked back in and the lid fell shut.

"I FOUND HIM!" Toby yelled excitedly. "About six hundred meters at eleven o-clock. Spider trap."

Riley regained his feet and sprinted to the bunker. As he did so, two more shots rang out in rapid succession--much too fast for a bolt-action rifle. And the sound of the report was too far away for and AK to fire this accurately.

He slid into the narrow doorway and grabbed the TA-1 field phone. He pumped the ringer rapidly and listened for a reply from the CP.

"CP," came the calm voice of Sergeant Alexander.

"This is Riley. We found the sniper. Can we get some mortar rounds out there?"

"Gimme the scoop."

Riley pulled his compass out, and with Galleon's assistance, pointed the azimuth wire toward the sniper's last position. "From my position, Oscar Tango Zulu two...seven...eight. Range...six hundred, over?"

"Understand two seven eight magnetic, six hundred mike, over?" Alexander read back the direction and range.

"Affirmative."

"Stand by, out."

"Toby, can you still see him?" asked Riley, looking for Mendoza's binoculars.

Galleon had kept his eye glued to the scope. "Naw, but I ain't seen him move either."

Just then sporadic firing broke out two positions west of Riley and Galleon. Toby looked up to see what that was all about and at that moment, Truong crawled out of the back of his hole, using the camouflaged lid to mask his withdrawal. Before the first mortar rounds impacted in the sand near the spider hole, Truong was safely out of range, using the short trees as cover.

"What the hell are you guys shooting at?" demanded Riley as he yelled down the line.

"I was returning fire," came the reply. it was the voice of Rawlings, the new guy.

"Cease fire until you get a target, dammit!" Riley turned back to the front. "Any luck, Toby?"

"Not yet."

The field phone clacked loudly and Riley picked it up. "Second squad, Riley here."

Alexander's familiar voice came back. "As soon as the mortars cease fire, I'm sending third herd out to flank the gook's position. Have your people cover their asses."

"No sweat. Listen man, I think we found our sharpshootin' gook."

Deitman's squad found an empty hole, and a few spent cartridge cases.

Examining them, Deitman turned one over in his hand. On the base was the marking "7.62 X 54". The case also was longer than the 7.62x39 millimeter AK-47 round, and had an odd protruding rim at the base.

"Check this shit out. This ain't no AK or SKS, and there ain't no way one of those old bolt-action jobs could crank off rounds as fast as this fucker did."

His partner looked at the empty casings. " What in the hell are they shootin' at us got now?"

"I don't know. But one thing's for sure. It beats the shit out of an M-16 for accuracy. Com'on. The Skipper will want to see these."

Chapter Twenty One

Mendoza came back to the bunker and peeked in sheepishly. "Miss me?"

"Yeah, where the hell were you when we needed you?" asked Riley.

"Man, you know how it is when you gotta make a head call," said the dusky Chicano. "I was over in the head when all the shit broke loose."

"You mean literally?" grinned Galleon.

"Yeah man, friggin' literally. What the hell happened?"

"Just a few pot shots from the best gook sniper in the world, that's all." Riley turned what was left of his canteen over in his hands. Three inches closer and he would have been minus one ass.

"Didn't look like pot shots to me man," said Mendoza also eyeing what was left of the exploded canteen.

"Well, until we find out what the hell is going on here, keep your ass low and stay outta sight during the daytime, understood?" instructed Riley.

"No sweat, man."

"Hey Riley?" asked Galleon.

"Yeah?"

"I ain't sure, but it sure looked like that gook was determined to zap your ass out there."

"Whatta ya mean?"

"Well, it wasn't like he didn't have plenty of targets. He just kept on you, compadre."

"I was wondering if it was my imagination or not. I was kind of occupied out there, ya know?"

"No shit, man. Wonder what you did to piss him off?" laughed Mendoza. "I know, maybe this dude don't like you so well cause you ain't no brother!" joked Mendoza, setting Riley up.

"What's that supposed to mean?"

"Well, figure it out. He didn't shoot at Galleon, he didn't shoot at me, he only shot at you!"

"I still don't get it."

"Mendoza? Galleon? Chicano man. Riley? Mick bro, just an Irish Mick!" Mendoza and Galleon both roared with laughter. It wasn't often they could throw around a bit of reverse discrimination.

Riley chuckled, but he was not one to be done by two such as this. "You may be right, beaners, but...just remember this," he paused for dramatic effect. "Just wait 'til the lads down at the I.R.A. hear about this bit of bloody nonsense." In his best Irish brogue, he had the last laugh. "Now ye wouldn't want to be goin' 'ome to find a wee bomb in yer bloody 'ouse, now would ye lads?"

"Shee-e-e-it." Mendoza shook his head.

"Shit is right," said Riley. "I just remembered something."

"What's that?" asked Galleon grabbing his rifle.

"I got a letter to mail," Riley answered, remembering the letter to Patty laying on the ground by the mail box.

"Watch your ass, man. There is a gook out there lookin' for your number."

All was ready for the attack on Hue, and the party was a double celebration. The planning staff of the North Vietnamese Army and the Vietcong, plus Major Dharkov, celebrated in the main chamber of the underground headquarters. TET had begun, and the plans were complete and approved. The units were in place, the ammunition and explosives issued, and everything appeared in order. Now they only had to wait for the designated time.

"Comrades!" The Battalion Commander of one of the Vietcong battalions that stood poised attack called for the attention of those gathered around him. "I propose a toast."

The assembled officers filled their glasses with rice wine. Dharkov wished it was vodka. "To...victory !

The glasses were raised in salute, then quickly emptied. The next commander toasted to Ho Chi Minh, and the next to the Revolution. And so it went until well after midnight. At one-o'clock in the morning, one of the NVA officers briefly excused himself. When he returned, he had several young Vietnamese girls with him. "Would any of my brave comrades like company tonight?" he laughed.

"Perhaps our comrade Major from the Soviet Union would like first choice," laughed a colonel, obviously showing advanced signs of intoxication.

Dharkov eyed the young ladies, wondering where they came from. Were they whores from Hue? Were they local village girls? "The Major from the Union of Soviet Socialist Republics respectfully declines the honorable Colonel's offer."

"Oh?   What is the matter, my friend? Perhaps you would rather have a young boy ?" The room reverberated with laughter. Dharkov did not find that amusing. His mind raced back to the young Korean girl that he had met in P'yongyang. Chiri Kangye was the daughter of a Korean lieutenant, and he had fallen in love with her. She too had been a revolutionary, but had died after an unsuccessful battle with tuberculosis. He had tried not to think of women since then.

She was one of the reasons he had volunteered for this assignment in Vietnam.

"Comrade Colonel, I do not find that amusing. It is late, and I wish to be excused. It will be a long day tomorrow."

"Our Russian friend is right. It is time we all adjourned. I also feel weary," said the senior regimental commander eyeing one of the girls. He took his choice by the hand and escorted her toward the tunnel that led to his chamber. "I will see all of you in the morning."

Truong could not believe that Buddha had forsaken him. He could only judge his failure as his own fault. The time must not have been right. He would wait two days and return to the Marines' camp. His mind analyzed each facet of his encounter and came to the conclusion that the fault was his own. All of a sudden, like a flash of light, he realized his mistake. He had slept safely in Buddha's temple, saw the idol and the incense sticks, but did not himself pray! "Forgive me, Father Buddha. In my haste I have forsaken your grace. I will make atonement at once."

He made his way in the darkness to a small village nearby and found a shrine. Laying Uncle Quan gently on the ground, he dropped to his knees and quietly chanted his prayers. He wished he could burn incense, but had none. Even if he had, he could not afford to show a lighted match in the night. A small flame could be seen for over a kilometer on a dark night such as this.

PFC Martin woke the Captain with a shake of his boot and a whispered "Sir?" He knew that you never touched someone who had spent time in the field anywhere else. It was too dangerous. They may come awake shooting or swinging.

"Yes?" replied the sleepy company commander.

"Radio, sir. Romeo one-zero wants 'Actual'."

"Regiment? Wonder what they want with me?" He sleepily got to his feet and crossed the room to the radio. "This is Bayonet two-niner Actual, over?"

"Two-niner Actual, this is Romeo one-zero, stand by to copy encoded message, over?" came the static filled voice.

"Send message, over."

"I shackel," began the voice, using the codeword for a message that had been encoded. "Delta, sierra, tango... india, november, xray..." and so the message went until all of the three letter codes were copied by the Captain. He read them back and confirmed them. After signing off, he opened his code book and deciphered the message. "Jesus..." he whispered, then "Gunny!"

The company gunnery sergeant had been standing just outside of the command bunker when the Captain called. He ran in the door to see what the commotion was about. "Something up Skipper?"

"Gunny, all hell has broken loose. The gooks have started a major offensive all over the fucking country!" The Skipper hardly ever swore. He was an officer, and he believed that officers should not swear, at least in front of the men. The

Gunny was an exception. Gunnery Sergeant Adams had been a Drill Instructor at Marine Corps Recruit Depot in San Diego for two years. After that he had become a Platoon Commander over a recruit platoon and three Drill Instructors. On his dress uniform he wore ribbons dating back to Korea. This was not his first experience with combat, or with Asians. There was very little that shook him up, and as an "Old Corps" career Marine, he feared no one. Especially the Vietnamese.

"What are they up to now?" The Gunny stood with his hands on his hips, an indignant scowl on his face. Fuck a bunch of gooks.

"They've evidently hit every major city in Vietnam. Saigon, Da Nang, Chu Lai, Hue and others. Da Nang isn't as bad as the rest, but Hue is catching hell. Since it is in 'I' Corps, we've been ordered to assist in a counter-attack. Seems the NVA and VC just ended the cease-fire."

"What about Khe Sanh?" asked the Gunny, his face beginning to cloud with concern. His son, Rick, was a machine gunner at Khe Sanh. He had joined the Corps to follow in his father's footsteps, and had just made corporal. He was the Gunny's only boy.

"I'm afraid Khe Sanh is catching it too, Gunny. I'm sorry."

"Rick will be all right sir, he's a good Marine."

"Sure Gunny."

The offensive had begun. Dharkov accompanied the 804 Battalion of the 4th North Vietnamese

Army Regiment. His Dragunov accompanied him.
They had spent the night in a river bed southeast of
the city, undetected.   Just before dawn, they
attacked.   Their objective was the MACV
headquarters on the south bank of the Huong River.
The resistance was less than expected, and victory
was almost assured.

While Dharkov was moving in on the
American compound, the 6th NVA regiment
attacked the west side of the city. This created a
pincer movement. Von Clauswitz would have been
proud.

The gunnery sergeant turned to leave the bunker.
The captain wanted him to fetch the platoon
commanders for a briefing.

"Gunny?"

"Yes sir?" He turned back to the Captain.

"One more thing. The 'Green Beanies' have
a Special Forces Camp at a place west of Khe Sanh
called Lang Vei. They have been hit pretty hard.
They are reporting tanks in the wire!"

"Tanks, sir?"

"Tanks, Gunny. Looks like they're serious
this time."

The gunnery sergeant grinned.   "Maybe
we'll finally get us a real stand-up fight this time,
Skipper, instead of just another sorry gook hunt."

"Looks that way, Gunny."

Truong spent the next night getting into position.
By morning he was ready.   When the sun
brightened the eastern sky, he scanned the hill of

sand. His heart sank. Buddha had once again forsaken him. The Marines, and Riley, were gone.

Chapter Twenty Two

Entering Da Nang was much more difficult now that the offensive had begun. Truong could not cross the bridges over the Cau Do for fear of being apprehended at a checkpoint, so instead he had had to transit the river at night by both wading and swimming until he reached the opposite bank. He had buried the Dragunov--carefully wrapped in plastic--on the far bank in a grave in a small Catholic cemetery. He memorized the words on the headstone so that he would be able to find it upon his return. The only weapon he took was a small dagger with a five inch blade. This he strapped to his right calf. It would be hidden by the trouser leg of his civilian pants that he had stolen from a village on his way to Da Nang. He had stripped to shorts, sealed his clothes in a plastic bag and crossed the river.

The main roads all held roadblocks manned by both American Marines and government troops. They searched or questioned everyone who wished to pass. Truong avoided these and the street patrols by keeping mainly to the alleys, smaller streets, and narrow foot passages between the ancient buildings. By mid-afternoon, he was in the narrow alley behind the old man's house. Without knocking, he tried the door. It was barred. Looking around, he noted several empty wooden crates. He stacked

these until he gained sufficient height to reach a
second story balcony. It was still early, and the
shutter doors stood open to the breeze. As quietly
as he could, he reached up, grabbed the rusty steel
railing and pulled himself up to the balcony. Soon
he was inside.

"Old man, I again need your help!" Truong
announced, awakening the white-goateed one.

"What? Who?..oh, it is you again. What is it
this time?"

"The same mission. I have less time now. I
need to see Diem as quickly as possible. Today!"
Truong was much more abrupt with the old one
now. It had been a long and dangerous night, and
with the offensive taking place, he was becoming
pressed for time. He had to find Riley before
something else happened to him. He had prayed to
Buddha for Riley's life! He felt odd, but it was he,
Truong, who must end it. Not some other comrade.

"It will be difficult to reach him. The san
bay is closed at all entrances and there are many
soldiers and police guarding the fences and gates."
The old man continued to describe the defenses of
the san bay, or airfield.

"I am sure one as wise as you can find a way
to deliver a message to him. When he is contacted,
tell him he must come today, and I will double his
reward." Truong had already given him all the
jewelry and gold that he possessed, and would try to
find a way to trick Diem into divulging the
information.

"Perhaps there is one way," smiled the old
one, remembering that he had a nephew who was a

QC, or military policeman. His nephew would be on mobile patrol today, and could deliver the message. He was loyal to the government, and suspected nothing. His uncle led him to believe that Dai-'uy Diem was an old friend of the family.

The company was inserted by helicopter in an open area between the village of Thanh Lam and Highway One. This was as close as the commanders wanted to get to Hue until they could organize their forces on the ground and get a better intelligence estimate of the situation. The reports from Hue, up to this point, had been sketchy and segmented.

Riley felt like "the cavalry to the rescue". His platoon grouped in a tree line on the east side of the LZ and waited. When the rest of the company had landed, the platoon leaders were summoned to the headquarter's element's location for a quick meeting.

"What's goin' on?" asked Karlov sitting down next to Riley. He felt much better now that he once again had his M-79 grenade launcher instead of the M-16 that jammed when he needed it. M-79s, which resembled a large single-barreled, stubby single-shot shotgun, do not jam. They simply break open at the breach and a round is inserted into the chamber. A quick flick of the barrel and the weapon was ready to fire. Karlov carried two bandoleers of forty-millimeter grenades that resembled huge bullets.

"We'll get the scoop when the lieutenant gets back, but I heard that we're supposed to link up with a convoy out of Da Nang as part of a reactionary force for Hue. We'll probably hump down this road toward the city when we get the word. From there, it's anyone's guess."

"Did you see Longarrow?" Karlov grinned as he thought of the Mohawk preparing for war before the movement.

"Yeah. He don't need to shoot any gooks, he'll scare 'em to death. It cracks me up when he puts on war paint!"

"He's got his tomahawk too!" Karlov leaned back against a tree trunk and took his helmet off. He remembered once in Okinawa how Longarrow had gotten them all thrown out of a bar in Henoko when he had gotten drunk and did a war dance on the table. The funny thing was that it only took two beers.

Riley looked over at Lamb and Foster. The salt-and-pepper team were in a much more serious mood today. They did not joke, and were busy going over their gear before the move out. Foster knew that he would be taking point on this one, and Lamb would be covering him as the follow-up. They didn't speak much. Each knew what the other was thinking.

Peewee walked over to Riley and dropped to one knee. "Sergeant Riley?"

"Yeah Peewee?" Riley noted a serious look of concern on the small Marine's face.

"There ain't gonna be any tunnels in Hue, is there?"

"I don't know Peewee. I kind of doubt it, though." Riley knew all about the cobra, as did the rest of the platoon.

"Man, I hope not." Peewee got up and walked over to Slacker and sat down. "Slacker?"

"Yeah?" Slacker had been trying to dial in AFRS radio on his little transistor. Finally he heard the familiar tune that seemed to play at least once each hour in Vietnam:

> "...These boots are made for walkin',
> and that's just what they'll do.
> One of these day's these boots
> are gonna walk all over you..."

Slacker looked down at his own boots, and said to himself, "That ain't no shit, Nancy. That sure ain't no shit."

Peewee patiently waited for Slacker's attention, and when he finally looked up, asked his question. "Slacker, are you afraid of snakes?"

"Peewee, the dude what says he ain't 'fraid of no snakes, is a lyin' muthah!"

"Thanks Slacker."

"Don' mention it."

Dharkov had not felt this good in years. Action took his mind away from his past, and this was indeed action. His group had hit the city hard, and even though they were now encountering more resistance, they had taken quite a bit of ground. Already units of his attack battalion were rounding up civilian prisoners. Most of the enemy military forces were performing a fighting withdrawal, but had left many dead behind in the streets. Dharkov was personally responsible for eight.

The NVA major walked up to the street corner where Dharkov peered around the edge of a building, looking for more targets. "Comrade Major, are you here to observe, or to fight?"

"It is hard to observe when one is this close without also fighting, is it not?" Dharkov dropped the scoped rifle from his eye and looked at the little Vietnamese whose face was shaded by his sun helmet with the red star emblazoned on the front.

"I do not complain, comrade. I am only concerned for your safety. I have instructions from the political officer that forbid me from allowing you to be captured. If that were the case, it would be better if you did not survive." The Vietnamese major had trouble finding the words to describe his orders. He had been instructed to not allow the Russian to become involved in the fighting, but it was proving extremely difficult. It seemed Dharkov had his own ideas. "Perhaps the Major would like to see some of our snipers in action?"

"Yes, of course." Dharkov grasped at the chance to get to a more advantageous position and knew that the NVA snipers would have just that. They would be using rooftops, second story windows and other places of high ground and concealment.

"Dai-'uy Binh will show you the way," said the little major. "I must attend to my men." The Vietnamese saluted and left, running quickly across the street to catch up with his staff.

Dharkov started off after the captain. Yes, it is good to be back in action....

Diem had difficulty excusing himself from the operations meeting, but had finally managed to give his part of the intelligence briefing to the air base defense commanders. As another officer began hanging another map in front of the seated officers to give a "sit-rep", Diem escaped. Now he once again sat in the old man's house facing Truong.

"Well, my friend, I am led to believe you have urgent need of my services." Diem mentally replaced the word urgent with the word expensive.

"I must know where the Americans have gone!" Truong had no time to waste playing games with the ARVN.

"What Americans?" Diem took his sunglasses off and placed them carefully on the table. His face appeared unworried, and he knew he had the advantage of one who could bargain with time. He could tell that Truong needed information. This was much more profitable than one who merely wanted it.

"Do not toy with me. I am very tired and I do not have much time." Truong wanted to get out of Da Nang and cross the river as soon as it became dark.

"Oh, you mean the Americans from the Temple of Five Dragons?" Diem lit one of his Vietnamese cigarettes, and exhaled a cloud of blue smoke. Truong coughed.

"Where did they go?"   The ha-si was growing impatient.

"I have just now come from a meeting that informed me where all the elements of the Americans are located at this very moment, and where they are going. I know of the unit of which you seek. However, the message I received said that I would be well rewarded for my knowledge. I do have many expenses in my line of work." Diem lied again.

"Yes yes," said Truong impatiently. "But first, the location!" He leaned forward on the table intently staring at Diem. He noted that Diem was wearing his Uncle Quan's ring.

Diem thought for a moment, then decided to give the information first. Had not Truong paid him before?

"The Americans you seek have just arrived south of Hue. They are to aid in a counter-attack. They will be entering the city from the south, and will try to re-take the 'Citadel'. That is all I know at this time. Now, about my fee?"

"You have all the fee that you will receive from me."   Truong stood and watched the expression on Diem's face change from one of impassiveness to one of disbelief.

"I do not understand. You must pay me for my services!"

"You already have all the valuables that I possessed. You will not see me again," Truong said quietly, never letting his eyes drift from Diem's.

"You have cheated me!" screamed Diem in an instantaneous fit of rage. "You cannot receive information without payment!" With this he grabbed at his holstered pistol and tried to stand.

Truong grabbed the edge of the table and flipped it toward Diem, blocking his actions. Diem managed to extract his pistol from it's holster. Just as he tried to level it, Truong dove into his chest, knocking him to the floor. Diem brought the butt of the pistol down on Truong's head, but was only able to deliver a glancing blow.

Truong reached down and gripped the knife strapped to his leg. The hardened ha-si would not mind killing a traitorous coward like Diem.

Diem was not easy prey, however, and the fight continued with each trying to gain control of the pistol as they rolled across the floor. The old man had long since escaped, and was hiding upstairs wondering how he would explain the commotion to the police if they came. Then a shot rang out.

Diem had tried to bring the pistol to bear on Truong with one hand while he kept Truong's knife hand locked with the other. But the young VC was strong, and before Diem could shove the pistol against Truong's body, his finger had accidentally pulled the trigger.

Truong fought desperately to control the gun. Diem hit him sharply in the nose with a left jab. The blow was so painful That Truong almost lost consciousness. For the first time Truong feared he might lose the fight. But the combination of pain and fear caused adrenalin shoot through his body, giving him the added strength to overcome Diem's struggles.

Truong could not afford another shot being fired. The police had probably already been alerted by the first one. The knife entered Diem's rib cage just above the third rib and penetrated his heart. Diem, his eyes wide with surprise, quivered briefly, then collapsed.

Truong pushed Diem's lifeless form off of his chest. He took Diem's pistol, stuck it in his waist band, wiped his blade on the dead man's shirt, and replaced it in the scabbard on his calf. It was time to go. He looked around the room and saw Diem's cigarettes. He picked the package up and walked back over to the still warm body. He pried Diem's mouth open and jammed the entire package between his teeth. "Here...you may need these where you are going." He then remembered his Uncle's ring, and twisted it off Diem's finger. After placing it on his own, he crawled out the back window. That is when he noted that the air was filled with many erratic rifle and pistol shots, marking skirmishes in various parts of the city. No wonder Diem's shot had not been heard.

After night-fall, Truong once again crossed the Cau Do.

Chapter Twenty Three

Hue was over fifty road miles from Da Nang and presented a definite problem to Truong. He feared he could not walk the distance in time to catch up with Riley. He knew from past experience that battles were very short, and the Marines had a nasty

habit of making them shorter. No one could guess
that the Battle for Hue would last a total of twenty-
six days.

The chaos of the offensive and its side
effects actually aided Truong in his efforts. People
were evacuating the areas around the battles, and
the roads were flooded with refugees. Families,
carrying what possessions they could, traveled by
foot, bus and cart to places of safety. On Highway
One, Truong joined one column of refugees fleeing
Da Nang for villages to the north, while another
column passed in the opposite direction to the
south. There was great confusion, and Truong used
it to his advantage.

After he had crossed the river and retrieved
Uncle Quan, he put on peasant garb and wrapped
the rifle and his equipment in a bundle of cloth. He
then cut green stalks of sugar cane from a small plot
and tied these around the hidden rifle.

He spent the first day making his way to the
north side of Da Nang to Highway One. Here the
highway winds through the mountainous Hai Van
Pass. Helicopters occasionally flew low along the
road, giving Truong a start each time they passed.
Once, one circled twice before continuing north.

Just before starting the climb up the pass, a
top-heavy xe-buy't bus stopped on the road ahead
and let off passengers. Truong hurried to catch up
before the bus could depart. Several peasants rode
on the roof amid a mixture of bundles, bicycles and
animals. Truong passed his own bundle up to be
placed in the cargo rack and climbed onto the bus.
If they came to a road block and encountered a

cuan-cu'c identification card check, Truong knew his student identification card would pass. He could only hope that the canh-binh would not check the bundles on the bus too closely.

The bus lurched forward in a cloud of blue exhaust smoke, horn bleating at the surrounding pedestrians. If the bus did not break down, and was not stopped by the military, Truong would be near Hue before dark.

The Marines moved forward in a tactical column. Two staggered rows of sweating troops used the sides of the road, creating knee-high dust clouds as they trudged forward under the weight of ammunition and supplies. The occasional jeep or Mighty Mite passed down the middle of the road in the opposite direction carrying wounded on stretchers, and occasionally, the inevitable body bag. If there was any thought that the enemy would run away before the company could get there, it was soon dispelled.

As Riley drew nearer the city, he could see columns of smoke rising from beyond the nearest roofs. Sporadic firing sounded from different directions, interspersed with the ragged staccato burst of machine guns. The squad passed two burned out ARVN trucks and a smoldering jeep. The wreckage looked perhaps a day old.

Gunny Adams turned around and faced the men behind him, walking backwards. "Listen up, girls," the gunny shouted. "The party's still on and we've been invited. We'll be entering the city in a few minutes, so watch your platoon sergeants and squad leaders. NCO's, keep us informed on your radios. We'll more than likely get separated in the buildings. I don't want nobody to get ahead of anyone. We move together!"

The company broke away from the rest of the column and started into the built up area called Hue.

"Comrade Major, comrade Duc is one of our best snipers. He has already eliminated four of the enemy." Dharkov looked at the young Vietnamese who smiled at him. The boy held an old Moison-Nagant bolt-action rifle with a newer Chinese scope attached. The long barrel still kept the weapon fairly accurate, and Dharkov credited the short ranges that the soldier was covering more than his skill, for his success.

Dharkov surveyed the scene and after a quick evaluation saw some things that needed correction. They were standing in a second story room of a concrete office-type building west of the Citadel. The building was at the converging intersection of three streets, with an open square below, and one could command an excellent view for almost two blocks before they curved out of sight. Dharkov could see the still bodies of two ARVN soldiers bloating in the street beyond the square below, apparently former victims of Duc's. Dharkov could also see that the youth propped his rifle on the window sill, with the barrel protruding out in plain view.

"Comrade Duc, it would be better to back away from the window and not allow any part of your weapon, or the discharge from it, to be seen from the outside. Take that table and push it near the window, then use some of this rubble for a rest. You can sit in a chair and watch the streets without the enemy seeing you. A sniper must conserve his strength. It is better to make the job as physically easy as possible, as it is mentally very demanding."

The boy quickly moved away from the window. "Thank you, Comrade Thieu-ta', I will correct my mistake immediately."

"I can see why you consider him one of your best, he obeys quickly," nodded Dharkov with approval. "Now I am sure you have more important things to do than escort me around. With your permission, I will stay here a bit more and observe this young warrior in action."

"Very well, comrade. If the battle draws close, I will return to move you to a new area." Dai-'uy Binh saluted and departed down the hallway. His steps could be heard crunching rubble on the staircase as he left. Now they were alone. Dharkov opened his thick canvas satchel and removed his Dragunov.

The bus stopped five kilometers from Hue and the driver refused to go any further. It is just as well, thought Truong as he retrieved his bundle from the rooftop rack. I will find the river and make my way into the city.

Ha-si Nguyen Van Truong walked west until he was out of sight of the road. Here he squatted in some brush and placed his bundle of sugar cane on the ground. Using his knife, he slit the reed cords that bound it and gently picked up the cloth-wrapped Dragunov. He carefully unwrapped it and used one of the rags to dust it off.

From a small pouch he pulled a tin of oil and began cleaning Uncle Quan. It would be dark in a few hours, and he would rest until midnight. He would spend the remaining hours of daylight going over his equipment; what was left of his bandoleer of 7.62x54 millimeter ammunition, his knife, a water bottle and a small bag of dried fish. He knew he could make these supplies last up to three days. The city should be able to provide more food and water, but he would have to use his ammunition sparingly. With Riley as his only target, the amount should prove sufficient.

He picked up Diem's pistol. It was a blue steel Smith and Wesson Model 10 .38 Special revolver. He thumbed the cylinder catch forward and opened the cylinder. He noted that he had only five rounds left. One had been fired during the struggle in the old man's house. He closed the cylinder and laid the weapon on a rag on the ground. He then fashioned a makeshift holster from a heavy rag and attached it to the belt taken from his civilian trousers. He buckled the belt above his waist and pulled his shirt over it. When he was satisfied with his work, he dug a small hole in the ground and buried everything that was no longer of use.

Truong thought of the tasks ahead. He did not know how he would find Riley, but he remembered that Riley's company would try to retake the Citadel. They would approach from the south, which narrowed Truong's search considerably. Truong chanted a long prayer to Buddha and decided that if it was to be, then Riley would be delivered to him. He found a level grassy place beneath a thorn bush and lay down to sleep.

"Riley, take your people up to the next street and wait there. You'll find a small park with a stone wall along one side. Set your men along that wall and sit tight. We got some ARVN's that should be here shortly and I'm gonna send you some to augment your squad. They know the area, and also know how far the other elements have advanced. I want Mendoza to stay back too. We need him for another team for the time being." Alexander reached for his radio handset and called for Deitman.

    "Okay, you heard the man. Let's go. Foster, take point. Lamb next, then Karlov," Riley ordered, lining up his squad. He fell in behind Karlov, with Galleon behind him, followed by Slacker and Peewee. Thomas and Simmons were pulled out by Hays to set up nearby to guard the CP against attack. Riley didn't like moving into action without his machinegun team, but it was their turn to provide security.

    "What about me, Sergeant?" Riley had almost forgot about Rawlings.

    "You got 'tail-end charlie'."

    The squad moved out, and as they rounded the next corner, saw a sight that was not rare in Vietnam. There, along the sidewalk, was a news team doing a stand-up. The cameraman stood in the middle of the street with his movie camera grinding away on his shoulder while the journalist stood on the sidewalk facing the camera, holding a microphone. Behind him was the only building that showed battle damage that the squad had seen so far. Everything else on the street was completely intact, and, other that the shots echoing in the distance, one would not know that a war was even going on. This particular building had a large hole in the front that appeared to have been made by a rocket round. Rubble and boards lay around the newsman and he looked around as he talked as if he expected to get shot at any second.

As the squad approached, Riley could hear him talking into the microphone. Riley called a halt to hear what he had to say.

"....and if there is the slightest doubt that the North Vietnamese are far from losing the war, one only has to look around. Here at Hue, it appears that the military has decided to destroy the city to save it. The battle continues to rage in every direction, and at this point it is anyone's guess how it will come out. American and South Vietnamese forces are almost at a stand-still at this time...."

Riley couldn't stand any more. He signaled the squad forward, and they passed between the cameraman and the commentator. Just as Lamb came abreast of the camera, he smiled a big Colorado grin and waved at the camera, yelling "Hi mom, having a great time at camp! Wish you were here!"

When Slacker passed, he showed his best scowl and gave the camera the finger. "Ain't shit happenin' man."

"CUT! CUT! Dammit, let's start at the top." The newsman stood there watching the Marines trudge off toward the park and waited for them to get out of sight for his second take.

Rawlings turned while they were still in vocal range and added; "Ya wanna see some real war, why don't ya come with us, pussy."

The ARVN patrol made their first mistake when they sent a scout across the street to recon the opposite side before proceeding. The British, the Germans and the Russians learned in World War Two that when you crossed a street from a position of cover, you darted across as a group. This surprised any waiting marksmen, and did not allow a sniper ample time to recognize and acquire a target until it was too late.

This patrol, on the other hand, waited for the single scout to check the opposite side of the street. Dharkov and his Vietnamese counterpart both saw the activity at the same time. The young NVA sniper drew a bead on the distant scout and was preparing to shoot when Dharkov stopped him. "Have patience. Soon there will be many targets. When I tell you, we both will shoot."

As the Russian had promised, the patrol leader began to send his men across one at a time. Three were across before Dharkov gave the order to shoot. "You take the three on the sidewalk. I will take the next one to cross. Fire after I do."

Dharkov let his scope settle on the center of the street and waited until the running South

Vietnamese soldier presented himself in his field of vision. When the target's body touched the right edge of the horizontal cross-hatch, Dharkov fired. His years of training and experience allowed him to judge the speed of the moving target and the lead. The ARVN threw his arms into the air and was lifted off his feet by the force of the impact of the bullet. Dharkov could see his prey was down in the middle of the street. As he had planned, the man was not dead.

A shot rang out from the old Czech rifle. One of the ARVN soldiers on the left of the street spun to the ground, his rifle clattering on the concrete. His two companions drug his body from view behind a pile of rubble. Then Dharkov's companion looked up with a grin, his look seeking approval.

"Not bad, but you still have two targets that you are responsible for," said the Major eyeing the scene through his scope.

"Yes, comrade Major, but it appears that you did not have such luck with your target. He still moves."

"As I wish him to do. One cannot catch a wolf unless one first ties a lamb to a tree." Dharkov did not look up. He was too busy concentrating on the street. "Watch."

Duc could see the slight movement of the wounded soldier and sat back to observe. Dharkov concentrated on the right side of the street. As he had predicted, the "bait" attracted the prey. The wounded soldier waved his arm in the air and pleaded for help. The two Communists could hear his screams, and it was not long before two small men ran to his aid. They each grabbed the wounded man's webbing and began dragging him to the safety of the building from which they came. Faster than Duc had ever seen, Dharkov fired two shots in rapid succession. Both men went down.

"Excellent! I have never..."

"Quiet!" Dharkov cut him short. He was still holding on target.

Now there were three men in the street. One was obviously quite dead, blood pooling in the street next to his head, but the last one to be hit was wounded. That left two as bait.

This time the ARVNs were not so hasty to retrieve their casualties. One brave soul reached his carbine around the corner of the building and fired several shots haphazardly down the street. Dharkov chuckled.

The Russian waited for two more minutes and then fired one shot at one of the wounded victims in the street, shattering his knee. He screamed in pain. Still no rescue attempt. Dharkov shifted to the first target and shot him in the hip, jerking him off the ground.

One of the ARVN soldiers who had previously crossed the street broke free of his cover and ran toward his fallen comrades, firing a Thompson submachine gun from the waist as he ran. The bullets ricocheted harmlessly off the street below.   Dharkov waited until he began dragging one of the casualties away and did not fire until he was almost to safety. Then he killed him.

"Why do you not just kill them and be done with it?" asked Duc, beginning to wonder about the Russian's sanity.

Without taking his eye from his scope, Dharkov whispered "If you would talk less and watch more, you would be much more effective."

"Soon they will have help, and it will be too dangerous to stay here." Duc was becoming worried. He knew that it was better to move after the first two or three shots.

"Leave me. Find another street to work, and I will work this one." Dharkov was again violating his own rules.

Duc left.

Riley's ARVNs arrived.   Three of them: an interpreter, his security man, and a soldier who had lived in Hue for several years. Everyone was being placed into action, and these three were no exception. They had been cut off from their unit when the offensive began, and were assigned to the Americans until the situation could be stabilized.

"Let's saddle up," said Riley standing up. "We'll move out now. Same march order."

The squad wound it's way through the streets until it came to an area exhibiting a larger degree of battle damage. The firing was close now. Riley deployed his people on a skirmish line and signaled them to take defensive positions. The sky was beginning to darken, and they would not be able to continue until daylight. Riley ordered a fifty percent watch, checked in on the radio, and settled in for the night.

Shortly after midnight, Truong entered the city. He was careful to avoid the enemy patrols by moving through the alley-ways and over roof tops until he drew close to the fighting. It was not as intense now, as each side was busy maneuvering for advantage in the cover of darkness. He decided to find a place of advantage south of the Citadel and wait for first light. By five o'clock in the morning, he had located an old French wine cellar with several small windows that looked out on an open square. The glass was broken in most of the windows. They would make good firing ports. He could move from one to another as needed, and the cellar had two routes of escape. One went into the alley behind the house and one was up the stairs to the floor above.

The early morning sun cast long shadows across the square, and Truong hoped that no one would come until later. The shadows made it difficult to see movement. Truong and Uncle Quan watched the square.

"Roger, out." Riley turned from his PRC-6 and faced his squad. "Toby, looks like you're needed. They got a sniper giving some ARVN's hell about four blocks from here. Six Actual is callin' for a counter-sniper and we're the closest."

"Okay, Jeff. Let's see if we can do a little better this time with this thing." Galleon stood and cradled the M40.

"Eddie, I want you close to me in case I need some instant artillery. This sounds like we could walk into an ambush, so load up with 'shot'."

Karlov popped the breach of the M-79 open and pulled out the HE grenade cartridge. He replaced it with one that contained hundreds of little steel balls. Now it was a forty millimeter shotgun.

The squad moved out cautiously, crawling around piles of rubble and burned vehicles. Within a block they could hear firing. Most of it was familiar thirty caliber carbine, with a few bursts of Thompson kicking in. When they arrived at the designated spot, they were greeted by a horrifying sight. Four dead ARVN's lay in the street and five more hunkered on the sidewalk beside a concrete building, obviously out of the line of fire. Across the street was one man hiding behind a pile of rubble. Riley's interpreter quickly exchanged words with the ARVN sergeant.

"What did he say?" asked Riley.

"He say they pinned down here all night. He say there beaucoup VC down street. He say they fight all night and lose four men."

Riley knew how they exaggerated, and figured that beaucoup VC meant maybe three or four. Still, there were dead soldiers in the street. "Okay, we'll take care of it. Toby, I'm gonna check this out, so just stand by. If we can spot the VC or NVA or whatever they are, we'll try to keep 'em pinned down until you can pick 'em off."

Riley took Peewee, Slacker and Rawlings and pulled back down the street. He wanted to move back a block and try a different street to approach the area that the ARVNs' indicated the fire coming from. After a detour around the block, they started inching their way back to the place Riley wanted to check out. Just as they drew close, a single shot rang out from their front and Rawlings was thrown to his face, his left leg bent above the knee.

"AWWW SHEEIIITTTT! JESUS....I'M HIT, OH MAN...."

Riley grabbed a purple smoke grenade from his suspenders and yanked the pin out. Guessing where the shot had come from, he threw it about twenty feet in front of Slacker who was running point and yelled, "Get back! I saw where the shot came from, let's move back!"

Slacker picked Rawlings up in a fireman's carry and Riley grabbed his rifle. Within minutes they were back with the rest of the squad.

"Okay, he's on that roof over there on the north side of the street. I don't know how he hit these ARVNs from there yesterday. He probably moved, and now can cover the other street better. Foster, Lamb, I want you to get upstairs in this building and pin the sonofabitch down until Toby can get in position. Slacker, get Rawlings back to the aid station and find a corpsman. One more thing, there's a small square that is wide open at the end of the street. You can just barely see it from here. Peewee, Toby, Karlov and I are gonna make our way to the opposite side of it where we can be ready. When you guys start firing at the bastard, we'll rush across the square and hit the building.

Once we get inside, there ain't no place for him to go. Got it?"

Lamb and Foster crawled through an opening where a window used to be and made their way to the roof to await Riley's signal. When Riley threw a green smoke grenade, they would spray the roof top at the end of the block.

Duc had left Dharkov, but had not gone far. He merely changed buildings and made his way to the roof. Laying behind a two-foot high concrete retaining wall, he waited all night. The first targets to avail themselves on the street below was Riley and his recon element.

He hit one of the Americans, but before he could work the bolt on his rifle and sight again, they escaped in a cloud of purple smoke. Now he waited for another target to present itself.

Truong could not see what the commotion was all about from his small sidewalk level window. The shot came from his left, and the purple smoke from his right. The activity was getting close, and he continued to watch the open square. He would wait for a few hours, then if there was no activity, he would move to a position of higher elevation. For the first time, the enormity of his task was beginning to seep into his mind. There were probably hundreds, perhaps thousands of Marines in Hue now. Should he waste any of his precious ammunition on others? He decided not. There was only one target that he wanted. And, thanks to Diem's information, he had to be near.

Chapter Twenty Four

Riley stopped just short of the corner and cautiously peered around the edge. He could see half of the square, and the building beyond where the sniper shot had come from. There was no way to tell if the sniper was still there until he fired again. Riley hoped that the sniper was still on the roof. If he had moved, then Lamb and Foster's suppressing fire would be useless.

"Toby, scan the roof and see if you can see anything."

Galleon, cradling the M40, edged up to the corner of the building. With the rifle against his left shoulder, he pointed it around the corner staying low to the sidewalk. "Naw, I don't see anything yet. He's probably staying out of sight if he's still there."

"Okay, let's think about this a minute." Riley pulled back from the edge of the building and sat down on the sidewalk behind Galleon. That is when he noticed a square concrete manhole cover by the curb. "Peewee, I hate to say this, but it's time to be a tunnel rat again."

"There ain't no tunnels around here," said Peewee nervously.

"Yeah, there is. Right here." Riley crawled over to the slab, and using his K-bar to pry up the edge, exposed a cavernous hole. They peered down and could make out steel rungs embedded in the side of the wall that descended into the storm drain system of Hue.

"Oh shit, man. What am I supposed to do in there?" Peewee pushed his glasses up on his nose and looked apprehensively at the opening.

"I want you to see if you can find a way to get over to the other side of the square and get into that building. If my guess is right, there should be more entrances like this on the sidewalk below that building. The sniper won't be able to see directly down from his position."

"Well, I guess if that's all the farther I have to go--" Peewee stripped his web gear off and held out his hand for Riley's pistol.

"Eddie, give Peewee your '79. Peewee, the blooper is loaded with buckshot. If anything gets in your way, just blast down the pipe and it will clear it out for about seventy-five meters."

Peewee took the short weapon and Karlov strung a bandoleer of 40mm buckshot rounds around his neck.

"Peewee, when you get over there, and if you can find a good place to come up, we'll see you. I'll pop smoke out in the square to attract the sniper's attention and Lamb and Foster will rake the roof to keep his ass down. You should be able to get into the building easy then. Watch your ass, and make your way to the second floor. I ain't sure if he's still there, so you'll have to check each floor. By the time you get to the second floor, we should be able to catch up with you." Peewee gulped, checked the M-79, slung it over his shoulder and entered the manhole. Riley watched him climb down the ladder, then closed the lid so that the sunlight would not silhouette the small Marine.

Karlov cursed as he stood back against the wall. "Goddamn it, I just knew it was gonna be a bad day!"

"What's the problem, Eddie?" Galleon asked without taking his eye from the scope.

"No sooner than I get rid of that 'McNamara's wonder' and get my blooper back, then I gotta give it up and get another piece-of-shit M-16!"

"Stow it, Karlov. It's only for a little bit, and Peewee needs the '79 in the tunnels more than we do up here right now."

Galleon spotted movement on the roof. "He's still there! I just saw a head poke up for a split second and then duck back down."

"Okay, as soon as Peewee finds his way over there we go. If he ain't there in fifteen minutes, we go anyway." Riley looked at his watch and marked the time.

Duc knew that something was about to happen. The Marines had pulled back too soon. They would probably be back, and he hoped it was not with tanks or the dreaded six-barreled ONTOS anti-tank vehicles. If one of those showed up, he would immediately leave. They could take down the whole building. He had no way of knowing that since he was this close to the Citadel, the tanks and ONTOS' were ordered not to participate. The Americans did not want to cause any political problems by damaging the ancient historical site.

The two foot wall around the edge of the roof would provide adequate protection against rifle fire, but if anything else was used he would make a hasty exit. He would wait a few minutes and scan the area again.

"I wonder where they are now?" asked Lamb.

"Dunno man. I ain't in no hurry though." Foster was laying unconcernedly on his back in the sun, his M-16 resting across his chest.

"I don't know if this fighting in cities is my piece of cake or not," remarked Lamb. "I kinda like bushes and trees to hide in. These green utility uniforms ain't exactly camouflaged for this shit."

"One thing about it, man, we ain't wading no rice paddies. My jungle rot is even startin' to dry up." Foster wished that they had time to take their boots off and let the sun bake their feet.

"Thirty-two more days and you can cook your rot on the beach in California. We're short, man. We're so fucking short that we need a step ladder to kiss a snake on the belly."

"It may as well be thirty-two years, man. We ain't outta here yet."

Peewee selected the concrete and brick storm pipe that led in the direction of the square and began his journey. For a change it was large enough to stand up in. He could walk upright, and this would cut a lot of time off his mission. He kept the M-79 pointed down the passageway and caressed the trigger every few steps.

There was six inches of stinking stagnant water in the bottom of the pipe, and his feet sloshed loudly as he walked. He couldn't do anything about that, and the noise was intensified as it echoed off of the walls in the long tube. Even his breathing sounded frighteningly loud.

Slimey dark green moss covered the walls, and cobwebs stretched across Peewee's face as he moved forward. Shivers ran up his spine as the thought of huge tropical spiders dropping on him in the dark crossed his mind. That's all the fuck I need now. Spiders and snakes!

Peewee was scared, but he wasn't terrified-- yet.

What was that? Peewee froze as he caught something moving in the shadows. He stopped breathing to listen. There it was again. Something moving in the dark, making very little noise. First ahead, then behind him. He began to sweat with apprehension. He carefully raised the huge muzzle of the M-79, knowing he only had one shot chambered. He could take out what was in front, or what was behind, but not both. Which way do I aim?

Then he saw what had caught his attention. Rats. The sewers were full of rats!

Oh shit! Wherever there's rats, there's snakes! Now Peewee was terrified. The charge of adrenalin surged into the pit of his stomach like a straight shot of Tennessee moonshine. I gotta get out of here! his mind screamed. But he could not go back the way he came. There were as many rats, and probably snakes, in that direction as the tunnel ahead. And his mission lay ahead.

He gulped, shook off a shiver of apprehension and pressed on, kicking water ahead to chase the rats away.   The drainage system had several openings to the gutters above and sunlight filtered down to illuminate small sections ahead.   All he cared about now was getting the hell out of there.

When he estimated he had gone far enough, he started looking for an exit from the subterranean maze.   Twenty-five meters further he came to another small room with steel rungs leading to the surface.   Peewee slung the M-79 and ascended the ladder as fast as his feet could find purchase.

It was time to leave the "safety" of the sewers, but Peewee did not care.   Man was an enemy he understood.   Spiders and snakes were not.

"There's Peewee!"   exclaimed Galleon as he spied the concrete slab near the building raise a few inches and then slide off to the side.

"Okay, let's do it."   Riley pulled the pin from the smoke canister, left the cover of the building and threw it as hard as he could.   It did not reach the square, but the cloud would rise above the roof tops and alert Lamb and Foster.   As it did, the familiar sound of the M-16s, firing bursts on full automatic, shattered the air.   The concrete retaining wall on the objective erupted in bursts of small white clouds as Lamb and Foster found the range.

Riley, trailed by Galleon and Karlov, sprinted toward the square.

Dharkov came alert at the sound of the firing.   He scanned the square and street to his front.   He could see nothing moving and wondered at the activity.   He could not see Lamb or Foster's position, nor could he see the roof to his left where Duc crouched. He knew better than to lean out of the window for a better view, and decided to continue his vigil on the area that he could effectively cover to his front. Patience, he thought.

Truong saw the Marines for the first time as they emerged through the cloud of smoke. They were running down the street toward him on the sidewalk opposite his vantage point. If he wanted to engage them, it would be easy. He would let them pass.

Lamb changed magazines as Foster took up the slack. They had to keep the volume of fire up until Riley's team was across the square and safely in the building. Foster ejected his empty magazine and Lamb rose to one knee to fire. After two quick bursts, his rifle jammed!

"Goddammit! Foster, this thing jammed. Cover them! He looked into the ejection port and saw that the weapon had tried to "double feed' two cartridges at the same time. He dropped the magazine from the well and held the cocking handle to the rear as he beat the butt on the deck. The cartridges would not come free. He pulled his bayonet from it's scabbard to try and pry them loose. Just then Foster's bolt expanded from overheating and froze to the rear of his smoking receiver.

Both weapons were inoperative.

RILEY! It was Riley! Truong saw the killer of Uncle Quan cross in front of him not more than thirty meters away!   The surprise of Riley's presence shocked Truong long enough to allow Riley's team to pass and enter the square. By then, Truong had recovered enough to bring the Dragunov into action. You will not escape this time, Riley.

He took aim, but Riley was not an easy target. The Marine zig-zagged every few steps, and never the same number as he ran. He was indeed experienced.   Truong decided to fire at the American to break his rhythm. The shot zipped in front of Riley and hit the radio suspended from his neck, jerking the Marine to one side. But Riley only increased his pace.

And what do we have here?   Dharkov grinned slightly as he saw the Marines enter the square below. Even a child could hit them. It is almost too easy. Dharkov stood and pointed his weapon down at the near side of the square and sighted in on the lead man. He fired just as Riley dodged to the right. He cursed his luck.

Dharkov fired two shots in rapid succession and saw the target and his two companions hit the ground, rolling away. They scooted behind a small monument in the square. Good. When you come out, you will die!

Peewee had made his way to the second floor and waited for Riley and the rest of the team. He could hear the shooting outside and noted the distinct sound of the Communist weapons. He began to wonder if anyone was still on the roof. He had heard no shots from above, and had mixed emotions on what to do next. Riley had told him to wait here, so he picked a small room near a staircase and waited. He once more felt very alone.

"Where the hell did that come from?" Riley asked as he tried to make himself as small as possible behind the base of the monument. There was no other cover in the little park, and they were trapped.

Karlov peeked around the edge and quickly eyeballed the buildings before jerking his head back. "I don't know. Our sniper must have moved!"

"Foster and Lamb ain't shootin'!" exclaimed Galleon.

Riley listened. Galleon was right. "Well, we can't stay here." He pulled the radio up to summon help and noted for the first time the neat bullet hole through the green aluminum case. "Radio's had it." He took it off and dropped it on the ground.

"Any ideas where the bastard is?" asked Galleon. "I need a target."

"No, but he has to be at the west side of the square somewhere." Riley remembered which way he had been jerked when the bullet struck his radio. "Eddie, spray that building to the west and Toby and I will try to make it across the square to Peewee. Maybe we can come through the buildings and hit him from the flank."

"Okay man. You ready?"

"Yeah, go!" Riley and Galleon started their sprint just as Karlov raised above the top of the pedestal's base and fired.

Dharkov had kept his scope on the monument and saw the American's head and shoulders. He fired. The bullet hit Karlov's helmet, blasting his camouflaged cloth cover open and knocking the helmet from his head. Karlov jerked backwards, his sightless eyes staring toward the blue sky. Dharkov then shifted to the two running Marines and fired again.

Galleon yelped in pain and fell to the ground, clutching his side. The flak jacket offered some protection, but the Dragunov bullet was only slightly deflected, striking him in the rib cage. He tried to crawl back to the monument, but Dharkov fired again. Galleon took the hit in his thigh and dropped the M40. Riley turned to look and ran back to his fallen comrade. In times of stress, the human mind does strange things. As Riley ran back to Galleon, two more rounds struck around his feet and a line from Kipling's Gunga Din crossed Riley's mind; "....with bullets kickin' dust spots in th' green...."

"Hang on Toby! I'll get you outta here!" Riley grabbed at the fallen Marine and at the same time picked up his rifle. He dragged him back to the monument and propped him against the concrete pedestal, next to Karlov. He looked at the body and immediately could see that the Mad Russian would fight no more. His face stared vacantly at the sky, his half open eyes looking like windows to a house where people no longer lived.   Jesus, Eddie...not you too!

He felt limp, confused and frustrated.   It wasn't supposed to happen like this.   He was supposed to bring them all through and take them all home alive.   It was his job.   He was their squad leader, their sergeant.   And now he had failed. Buth then he though of the enemy, the gooks, the bastards who had done this.   And they were still out there.   Killing Marines.   Killing his Marines.

Anger filled him.   And a sense of revenge. And a sense of survival.   He had to find the gook that had done this, who was keeping him pinned down, and kill him.   He had to kill him for Eddie Karlov, and maybe for Lamb and Foster, too.   And he had to save both himself and Galleon.   He choked back his emotions, and picked up Karlov's M-16.

Carefully sliding around the side of the monument, he raised the weapon and emptied the magazine in four bursts at the two suspect windows. He crawled back to Karlov's body and jerked open a magazine pouch on his belt.   He pulled out another magazine, jammed it into the M-16, and crawled back to the monument.   He eased up over the edge, sighted in on the windows and pulled the trigger. After three rounds, the weapon jammed.   He threw it down and picked up Galleon's sniper rifle.

Dharkov jumped back as the M-16 bullets exploded off of the ceiling over his head.   This allowed his two victims to regain sanctuary.   He crept back up to the window and settled his scope on the monument.

NO! You cannot have them! Truong's mind screamed in frustration. Riley was his! He could not gain effective access to the Marine's location from his present position and quickly realized he had to move. He ascended the steps two at a time and found a room that offered a better view of the square. There was a hole in the wall that had been made by a large piece of shrapnel, and it would be less obvious than the window. He elevated Uncle Quan and sighted in on the monument. Now Riley. Come to me now!

Duc made his decision. It was time to leave his position on the roof. He slung his rifle and began to crawl along the edge, keeping behind the short wall. When he came to the opening to the roof, he entered and descended the steps.

Peewee heard someone coming. He stood close to the door and listened as the footsteps crunched in the debris of broken stone and concrete dust. He could tell it was someone coming from the roof. He waited. Then, as the sound of the footsteps changed to those of someone walking slowly down the hallway, Peewee stepped out and faced Duc.

Duc was surprised, but recovered quickly and tried to bring his rifle to bear. The M-79 was already pointed at him.

The thought of trying to take the NVA prisoner entered Peewee's mind for a fraction of a second, but when he saw the rifle being elevated, he fired.

The mass of steel pellets struck Duc and blew him backwards onto the stairs. He was dead before he hit, his body turned to hamburger.

Lamb finally dislodged the stubborn bullets from the chamber of his rifle and reloaded. Foster had field-stripped his M-16 and was cursing as he beat it against the roof. Lamb sighted in on the target building again and fired a burst. But Peewee had already eliminated his objective.

Riley tore Galleon's battle dressing from its pouch and placed it against the wound in his side. He took his own and wrapped his bloody thigh. "Toby, we can't do anything from here. I gotta get over into those buildings and do something about that sniper." He crawled over to Karlov's body and took his last full magazine from his belt. After retrieving the M-16, he jammed the magazine into the well with a resounding "click". Working the charging handle, he handed it to Toby.

"One magazine and you're out of it. Use half of it to cover me while I get to that building. When I clear it I'll be able to get some help." Riley picked up the M40 and got ready to run.

"Watch your ass, Riley. Anything happens to you and I'm dead meat out here. There probably ain't another Marine within blocks of this place," said Galleon as he crawled painfully to the edge of the monument.

Riley looked at him and gave him a thumb's-up. "I'll do my part, you do yours."

Galleon leaned around the side of the pedestal and fired two five round bursts at the windows while Riley sprinted to the door of the building. Once he was inside, Galleon leaned back against the wall. Good luck, Jeff. He then passed out from the pain.

Truong could not get a shot at the running Marine as the sprinted across the open. He moved too quickly and zig-zagged as he went. But he saw him disappear below his vantage point into the next building. He had come far to find Riley, and now Riley had found him. It was time to close the gap that had eluded him for so long.

He quickly checked the magazine on the Dragunov, then pulled away from the hole in the wall to make his way to the ground floor. He moved quickly, but quietly. It was much easier to move on these concrete floors, even though they were littered in places with debris, than through the jungles or rice paddies. This should be easy.

He stopped at the ground floor and peered cautiously around. Except for broken furniture and a worn tapestry that hung on a wall, it was empty. He crossed the room, staying below the windows, and found a rear entrance to the building that led to a narrow roofless passageway. Across the passageway was a door that entered the building that held his prey. He darted across and dove through the door to the floor.

Dharkov knew that fighting at close quarters was not what a sniper did best. He grabbed his weapon and ran out the door. The Marine would be on the floor below, and would probably be looking for him. He had anticipated such a predicament and had planned his escape accordingly. By locating a window at the rear of the building during his exploration of the sniper's nest before the action began, he had ensured his survival. It provided an excellent escape route, with easy access to a dead-end alley one floor below that ran almost the length of the block, and offered him his next hide with good fields of fire with a minimum of movement on his part. Exactly what an experienced sniper required. He crawled through and dropped to the alley, scanned quickly left and right, then ran to the end nearest the street opening.

Sliding to a stop behind the abandoned hulk of an ancient Citroen that rested on it's brake drums near the street, he brought the Dragunov to bear over the rusted trunk deck and drew the scope to his eye. From the rear bumper of the car, he could see well through the missing back window and front windshield frames. The roofline and door posts that framed his position would hide his form. Here, he could wait for the Marine to search the building and hopefully step into the alley. Ambush them when they feel the fighting is over. Dharkov fell back on doctrine.

Riley held the scoped rifle. It was better than his pistol, but he longed for his M-14. He slowly ascended the stairs and checked the hall. It was empty. Room by room he searched the rest of the floor. When he came to the room overlooking the square, he saw the table and the spent casings from the Dragunov. He recognised the markings and the lipped rim as the same type that Deitman had brought back from the spider hole at the base camp outside An Hoa. Whatever the hell is shooting these things is Goddamned accurate.

A horrible thought occurred to Riley. Could this be the same sniper that was so intent on getting him back an An Hoa? Naw...couldn't be. Not so far from Da Nang.

Shaking the thought from his head, Riley searched the rest of the floor. Finding nothing, he started back down the stairs.

Truong heard footsteps and slid back into the shadows against a wall. It had to be Riley. A satisfied grin creased his face as he realized that he would be able to see the fear in Riley's eyes just before he killed him.

The footsteps stopped at the bottom of the stairs. Truong could not tell exactly where his victim was, but knew he was near. Very near. He felt the safety lever on his SVD with his forefinger. Satisfied that it was in the down position for fire, he waited.

Riley looked up and down the hall. If the sniper had just left, where could he have gone? Across the hall was an open doorway--the only room he had yet to search lay beyond. Riley quickly crossed the hall, stopped next to doorway and placed his back against the wall. Removing his last grenade from his belt, he pulled the pin and tossed it in.

The explosion shook the building, jarring loose ceiling plaster and filling the hall with the acrid smell of burnt composition B. Riley quickly stepped into the room, rifle at the ready.

Sunlight stabbed into the room through a single window. It was open, the shutters standing wide. Riley crossed the room and peered out, careful to keep his silhouette in the shadows. Below was an alley, across which was another row of ruined buildings. It was obviously the way the sniper had escaped.

Riley studied the alley. Directly across was a cluster of steel drums overflowing with trash. He would be able to run across and hide there while he surveyed the area. He wanted to make sure the sniper was gone before returning to Galleon and Karlov.

He readied himself, gripped the rifle tightly, crawled through the window and raced to the protection of the drums.

Truong heard Riley leave. He once again went through the door to the outside passage and crept to the alley. At the corner he could see a block in either direction. At the north end was an old car, at the south was a dead end. Halfway between the two was a collection of refuse drums, trash and rubble. It would be better to find his way though the buildings to the dead end to make sure he could cover the entire length of the alley. He did not want Riley to come up behind him when he finally exposed himself. Truong turned and disappeared into the ruins.

Dharkov saw Riley cross the alley and dive behind the barrels. He sighted in and waited. As soon as the Marine appeared again, he would die.

Riley found a narrow gap between two barrels and leveled the rifle down the alley. He drew the scope to his eye and examined the car. Noting nothing unusual, he rose to look the other way. He had just risen high enough to clear the tops of the drums and boxes when he was struck by Dharkov's bullet. His left shoulder exploded in pain. The bullet was high, striking below his collar bone, and breaking a rib just above his lung. He fell to the ground, his left arm useless.

Truong was shocked at what he had just witnessed. He had just filled his scope with Riley's body when Riley went down. The sound of the shot identified the assailant as one of his own. "Do not shoot! This one is mine!" screamed Truong down the alley.

Dharkov heard the words and hesitated, wondering who it could be. Did the Marine know Vietnamese?

"Your tricks will not work, American. You will die in this place!" Dharkov yelled back in Vietnamese.

"I am a ha-si with the National Liberation Front. If you do not have a higher rank than I, leave me this kill!" Truong returned.

"Then he is mine! I am Major Talanin
Dharkov of the Soviet Army!"

Truong recognised Dharkov's voice and was
incredulous at his appearance in the battle zone.
"Comrade Major, it is I, Truong. I have tracked this
American far, and I wish his life."

Riley could not understand the exchange,
but knew that he was caught between two enemies.
This is the story of the great war that Rikki-Tikki-
Tavi fought single-handed...

Riley was trapped, alone. His wound prevented
him from trying to escape back through the window
across the alley, and he wondered if someone would
come looking for him. Where was Peewee?

"Riley!" shouted Truong. He spoke no
English, but he wanted Riley to know that his
assailant knew who he was.

What the hell? How does that gook know
my name? Recognition hit Riley like a blinding
sunrise. This has gotta be the gook from An Hoa,
but why is he after me?

Feeling that the one behind the old car was a
greater threat at the moment, Riley picked the rifle
up with his good arm and layed it across a pile of
stinking rags piled in the narrow gap between the
two drums. He leveled it on the old car and then
lowered the barrel to the pavement below. He
would try skipping a shot underneath. He fired and
the bullet bounced off the hard surface and flew
past Dharkov's left boot. Dharkov jumped.

Riley had to lower the Model 70 and cradle
it against the rubbish to work the bolt with his good
hand. He jacked the bolt back, sending the spent

brass casing flying into the rubbish, then jammed it forward, chambering a fresh round.

Peewee heard the shots and made his way to the bottom floor of his building. From there he found an exit to the rear and came out onto a street. The shouting drew his attention, and he started trotting in the direction of the voices. As he approached the mouth of the alley he spied a uniformed figure crouching behind a rusty automobile.

Dharkov heard someone running down the street behind him and spun to see who it was. The sight of the Marine running toward him startled him. He quickly shifted his weapon to bear, and without sighting, fired three shots in rapid succession.

Peewee felt one bullet graze his hip and yelped in pain. He dodged into an alcove and slammed his back up against a wall. Breathing heavily, he quickly checked his wound. Blood seeped slowly around the ragged edges of the hole in his trousers, but he could see that, though painful, it was a minor graze and would require no immediate attention. "You son of a bitch," he cursed under his breath as he eased the safety off his M-79.

He inched around the corner to try for a shot. But as he raised the M-79, Dharkov squeezed the trigger of his SVD.

Dharkov's bullet hit Peewee's M-79, penetrating the side of the action, jamming the trigger. It could not be fired. The jacketed round then took a new direction and hit Peewee above his right arm pit, lodging in the joint. Peewee spun to the ground.

This time, the wound was much worse. The pain quickly swelled until it was almost unbearable. But Peewee knew that only seconds separated him from death. His assailant could easily end his life with one more trigger squeeze. He played dead.

Peewee counted to fifty. Nothing happened. He fought back the pain long enough to roll the few feet back into the alcove.

Propping himself up against the wall, he took stock of his situation. He was bleeding from both his hip and his right shoulder, his right arm hung useless at his side, and even if he could use it, he had no weapon. Peewee had lost his will to fight, and whoever it was at the end of the alley could, at his leisure, walk down the sidewalk and pump bullets into him--and he could do nothing about it.

Riley shifted the crosshairs to bear on Truong's position. He was losing blood and knew that it was only a matter of time before he lost consciousness. His only battle dressing had been used on Galleon, and if he was to survive this alley of death he had to find some way to stop the bleeding. He looked around. His only salvation would lay in the pile of dirty rags scattered about him. Gritting his teeth to keep from crying out, he painfully laid the scoped rifle across a wooden crate and picked up a piece of tan cloth that appeared relatively clean. He tore it into a long strip and bound his shoulder as well as he could. It would have to do.

Riley drew the scope back to his eye. The VC who had called out his name would have to expose himself sooner or later. And when he did, this time Riley would be ready.

How did he know my name?

Truong eased the edge of his head around the corner, exposing just enough to see his opponent's position. Riley fired.

The bullet creased Truong's head above his left ear and blood began to flow down his face, running into his eye. He slapped his hand over the wound and threw himself back against the wall. No prize came easy. He blotted his eye on his sleeve and dropped to his knees. He would have to be more careful.

Dharkov was determined to kill Riley. It was his only escape. He knew that he had hit the Marine in the street behind him, but did not know how incapacitated he was. If the American was still effective, he blocked his exit--and freedom. Dharkov was being distracted by having to watch in two directions for targets and danger.

He had to lure out the one in the alley.He had to make the American trust him. The only way to win that trust was by killing Truong. It was unfortunate, but in war, sacrifices must be made. He cupped his left hand beside his mouth and yelled "Hey buddy, are you an American?"

Riley couldn't believe his ears. Could it be that he was shot by friendly fire? He shouted back,

"Hell no! I'm a Marine, you stupid son of a bitch! Who the hell are you?"

"Smith...Sergeant Smith. I am sorry. I thought you were the enemy." Dharkov hoped his English was sufficient.

"You shot me, you crazy fuck!"

"It was an accident. Listen carefully. I will fire at the Vietcong while you come this way. Wait until I shoot." Dharkov sighted in on the far end of the alley.

Truong heard the exchange of words in English and quickly looked around the corner. Since blood continued to blind his left eye, he had to expose more of his body to see with the remaining good one.

Dharkov's bullet slammed into his chest, throwing him onto his back, a neat hole in his chest. Uncle Quan skittered across the alley.

"Come quickly! I have hit him!" yelled Dharkov, shifting his aim to the trash pile.

Riley saw the VC laying in the alley and weakly stood up. He took three steps and fell to the ground.

Dharkov watched and grinned. He knew that he had hit the American, but wasn't sure how badly he had been wounded. But he felt confident that his victim would pose no threat to him if he left the cover of the car. He always enjoyed the final moments of the kill, when he could see the expression on the victim's face when they knew death was imminent. And the closer he could see it, the better. It was one thing to be a sniper, who killed at long range, and quite another to be a predator. A stalker. A killer. For to Dharkov, there were two types of animals in the world: meat eaters, and grass eaters--grazers and hunters. Dharkov was definately a hunter.

Dharkov left his refuge and walked slowly to the still form in the alley to finish his kill.

Truong blinked. He was still alive. The initial shock of being struck by Dharkov's bullet had subsided enough to permit consciousness to return. Now he had two enemies to contend with. Moving very slowly, he painfully began inching his way toward Uncle Quan.

Dharkov stood over Riley and noted with satisfaction that the American was still conscious. He had lost a great deal of blood, but his eyes looked up and recognition changed his expression as he saw the Russian's uniform.

Dharkov aimed the Dragunov between Riley's eyes and smiled.
"Sometimes you Americans can be very trying, my friend. You have fought well, but not well enough."

Riley closed his eyes. It was over, and he would die in some shit-hole back alley in a shit-hole city no one had ever heard of.

Dharkov kicked him. "Open your eyes, dog! I want you to see this!"

As Dharkov looked down at the wounded American, Truong used the diversion to retrieve Uncle Quan.

Dharkov had shot him! Why? Truong had the strength for one shot. He rolled over, brought the weapon to his shoulder, and fired.

Dharkov's back exploded in an eruption of red mist and flesh. A questioning look transformed his face from one of satisfaction to one of surprise. Then his hands jerked in reflex, pulling the trigger.

The Dragunov discharged in a blinding flash and a shattering concussion of muzzle blast. The heat singed Riley's face and the explosion shattered his right eardrum. But the muzzle had been pulled away from Riley's head when Truong's bullet struck Dharkov. The bullet, slamming into the pavement next to Riley's face, ricochetted harmlessly away.

Riley could not believe he was still alive. For one brief moment, his would-be killer stood over him, grinning down with a death's-head face, ready to end his life at leisure. Then the next second he was gone.

Riley stared up at the blue sky, noting some wisps of smoke drifting by from something burning in the distance, then a small flock of white birds as they crossed his field of vision, fleeing some perceived danger. The ringing in his ear silenced the distant chatter of machineguns, the roar of jets passing, and the staccato beat of helicopter rotor blades. The war continued all about him, but he was oblivious to it.

Finally, he rolled over and struggled to his feet. He looked down unsteadily at Dharkov, then over to Truong. Picking up the rifle, he staggered toward the Vietnamese.

Truong watched him approach, but the rifle he held was too heavy to raise again. He could only watch. Uncle Quan, I will be with you soon...

Riley stopped short of Truong and surveyed the scene. The odd looking Dragunov drew his eyes. That's a long barreled sonofabitch for an AK...and a goddamned scope to boot! Recognition spread through his mind as he noted the long brass case of the expended Dragunov cartridge with the lipped rim laying on the ground near by. Riley's attention shifted back to the form at his feet.

He stood swaying dizzily over the small Vietcong and tried to decide what to do next. He tried to elevate the barrel, but found it too difficult to bring to bear with his one good arm. He then tried to cradle the heavy rifle in his limp left arm, but it refused to cooperate. Placing the butt against the ground, he leaned the barrel against his belt and clumsily drew the forty-five. I can't miss from here!

Truong watched in silence as the huge barrel of the pistol rose to his face. He was not afraid. If Buddha wanted him, then nothing would change that.

Riley looked into Truong's un-bloodied good eye. "How did you know my name?"

Truong could not answer. He did not know what Riley had said. Riley looked around the alley. They were alone. All about him the battle raged, but Riley's war was in this alley. It was not in the next street, or in Da Nang, or Saigon. It was here. And it was now. The contest was about to end and he was going to be the victor.

He looked down the length of the Colt's slide, leveling the sights between the small Vietnamese's narrow brown eyes. Squeezing the slack out of the trigger, he concentrated on holding the quivering pistol still for the final shot that would end his enemy's life.

He had killed many men, but none so close as to see their face, to see their eyes watching him, as he pulled the trigger. He knew that of all the memories of the war that would stay with him for the rest of his life, this one would haunt him the most. Could he live with the thought of shooting a helpless man, watching his head explode against the concrete, scattering brains and blood in a cloud of flesh and bone? Riley's emotions were torn in two directions. This Vietcong was his enemy. But for some reason, his enemy had just saved his life. A verse from Kipling sprang into his foggy mind.

> "Oh East is East, and West is West,
> and never the twain shall meet,
> Till Earth and Sky stand presently,
> at God's great judgement seat.
> But there is neither East nor West,
> Border, nor Breed, nor Birth,
>   When two strong men stand face to face,
> Though they come from the ends
> of the earth!"

In the well-worn words of the American fighting man in Vietnam, Riley summed it up with his statement to the Vietcong, even though he knew the VC wouldn't understand the words. Somehow it didn't seem to matter.

"It don't mean nothin', man. It just don't mean nothin'."

Riley clicked his safety on, holstered the pistol and looked around. Soon the fighting would pass this place, and this young one would be out of danger--if he lived.

Riley knew that his own wounds would at least remove him from further combat until his rotation date arrived, if not get him medevaced to the States immediately. Killing this kid would mean nothing to anyone. He was already effectively neutralized.

He dragged Truong down the alley and placed him between the trash barrels. He quickly covered him with rags and papers, leaving only his face open to the air. This done, he pulled out one of his canteens, unscrewed the lid and gave Truong a drink.

Screwing the lid back on, he laid it next to the Vietcong and stepped back. "Gotta go. Maybe your friends will find you. Maybe, just maybe, we'll both make it home."

With that Riley turned, picked the Model 70 up by the sling and stepped across Dharkov's body to leave.

Truong eased Diem's Smith and Wesson out of the make-shift holster under his shirt. The front sight came to rest between Riley's shoulder blades and he took the slack out of the trigger.

"Riley..."

Riley stopped. He turned back to look and saw the black revolver pointed at his chest, not more than ten feet away. There was nothing he could do.

For an eternity the weapon wavered. Truong's face was clouded with confusion, his mind with a mixture of feelings. Riley had the chance, but did not kill him. Why?

He lowered the pistol and dropped his head back to the pile of rags with a sigh. "Di-di, Riley...di-di mau..."

Riley turned and walked down the alley.

Chapter Twenty Five

The radio announcer had predicted a hot day. Riley felt like he was freezing to death. Since arriving stateside a week ago, the temperature had not risen above eighty degrees. On the day Riley had been medevaced from Da Nang, the heat hovered at over a hundred and twenty degrees. The forty degree difference brought a shiver to his tropics-shrunken frame.

After a week at NSA--the Naval Support Activity Hospital at China Beach at Da Nang--he had spent four weeks in the surgery ward in the hospital in Yokosuka, Japan, before being flown home. Now he was a "re-hab" patient in Balboa U.S. Naval Hospital in San Diego, the closest military medical institution the Marines could get him to home. For Riley it was like being right next door. Patti, and his parents, had come down from Huntington Beach to visit him three times already, and were now busy at home preparing for his upcoming convalescent leave. Spending twenty days away from the "Green Machine" was going to be great, but the foremost thing on Riley's mind was the back seat of his '61 Impala, the drive-in theater, and Patti. Hopefully, if the faceless clerks who typed the orders that dictated mens fates didn't screw up, his leave would start this weekend.

Today was the first time he had been allowed to leave the hospital grounds, and he was taking advantage of it. With his liberty card in his pocket, he had caught a ride downtown with a lance corporal in a Marine pick-up on his way to Marine Corps Recruit Depot on a supply run.

The heavy dress green uniform felt funny. Much too tight. And the lack of bill on his garrison cover, dubbed a "piss cutter" for some reason never explained, or forgotten, provided no shade for his eyes. He stood on the sidewalk and looked up and down the street. He still could not get used to a place that did not have booby traps, snipers, and ambushes. And it was odd, after nightfall, to not see a night sky streaked with the fiery path of green and red tracers and illuminated by the familiar pop and sizzle of parachute flares. And every time he saw a group of people standing together, he fought the urge to scream: "Break it up, idiots.   One grenade will get you all!"

He walked down the sidewalk, passing the familiar sights of locker clubs, bars and tattoo parlors. Pausing in front of a storefront window, he admired the two rows of ribbons above his left breast pocket. Though partially hidden by the sling that supported his arm, he could still plainly make out the bright yellow and red Vietnam Service Ribbon and the white bordered purple ribbon that denoted the Purple Heart.

He turned and looked down the street toward the waterfront. It seemed like a million years since he had boarded ship at Broadway Pier for Okinawa. It was like a dream, now. Or maybe a nightmare. And it was fantastic, surrealistic, and incredible--like it had never happened. Or if it did, it was in another life, with another Riley. One who was much younger and different than the one who now stood on the sidewalk watching the people with the innocent and naive faces pass by. They would never understand--probably wouldn't even care-- what was going on across that placid blue ocean that lapped the shores only a few blocks away.

Then his subconscious mind took over and the faces came. All of the guys who shared the danger, the excitement, the fear in that land of a different world. Some were dead now, but most were still alive--somewhere. Foster and Lamb had found Peewee after coming down off their roof to catch up with the squad. He had lost a lot of blood, but they got him to a temporary Battalion Aid Station in time to save him. Galleon stayed with

Karlov's body until another squad found them in the square--Marines never leave their dead behind. And Slacker Burnett, who had stopped briefly to visit Riley at the Naval Support Activity Hospital at China Beach, back at Da Nang told Riley that he had inherited the remnants of the squad. And now he had to carry a fucking pistol. And he damned sure didn't like the track record of squad leaders in second squad. "They promote you, then you get dinged or zapped," lamented Burnett. "It just ain't fair, man."

Then there was that gomer in the alley. Riley could see his bloody, pain-wracked face as if it were before him now. Wonder what ever happened to him....

Then he shook the thoughts away like shrugging off a field pack that was much too heavy and had been carried far too long.

"Lighten up, Riley," he said to himself as he turned to walk down the sidewalk. "It don't mean nothin'."

It was time to fulfill a promise he had made to himself in Vietnam. For twelve months he had craved anything that was cold. Ice Cream, cold milk, milk shakes, even ice cubes. For the grunts there was nothing that could be had that was cold. Even the beer, delivered two cans per day when the helicopters could find them, was hot. Now Riley would accomplish his mission. He would search out a bar and destroy a beer. A cold beer. Nothing else in life at that given moment was more important.

The sign in the window proclaimed the place as The Anchorage. Sounds from a juke box could be heard from the sidewalk. Riley walked in.

He navigated his way through the darkened interior past sailors playing pool, Marines leaning against the bar swapping sea stories in boisterous voices, and rough looking dock workers who sat glumly in the shadows swilling beer in moisture-covered mugs. He located an empty booth, slid in and waited for the bar hop. Within a few minutes she walked over, picked up two empty glasses and wiped the table. "Whatta ya have, Marine?"

"What ever you got on tap, as long as it's cold."

"I'll have to see some I.D," she said, surveying his young looking face. She studied his eyes and noted that he may not be as young as she first thought.

Riley had not even thought about it. Here in the States, there was a drinking age. He pulled out his water buffalo-skin wallet and produced his green I.D. card.

"You got a driver's license?"

"I used to, but it's in some rice paddy in Vietnam."

She scrutinized the plastic covered card and located the "Date of Birth" block. She handed it back. "Sorry sonny, you aren't old enough to buy beer."

Rage began to seethe inside Riley. He was old enough to be a Marine, old enough to fight for his country, old enough to kill, and old enough to get killed, but not old enough to buy a frigging beer.

"Listen lady...."

"I don't wanna hear it, jarhead. We can't afford to get busted for serving a minor. It's too damned hard to get a license to give it up for that. Now un-ass the premises before I call the Shore Patrol."

Riley slid out of the booth, crossed the bar and started to walk out the back door to the alley. He stopped short when he opened the door. It had been only a few short weeks since he had been in another alley. No more alleys for this lad.

He turned and headed for the front door.

He paused briefly at the door, turned and looked back at the patrons in the bar who took little notice of the gaunt Marine with his arm in a sling.

Riley rubbed his shoulder, turned and walked into the sun.   Then the words came:

"I went into a public-'ouse to get a pint o' beer,
The publican, 'e up an' sez "We serve no red-coats here..."
The girls be'ind the bar they laughed and giggled fit to die,
So I outs into the street again an' to myself sez I:
...For it's Tommy this, an' Tommy that, an'
"Chuck him out, the brute!"
But it's "Saviour of 'is country" when the guns begin to shoot;
An' it's Tommy this, an' Tommy that, an' and anything you please;
An' Tommy ain't a bloomin' fool,

you bet that Tommy sees!"

Rudyard Kipling
"Tommy"

-THE END-

Other books by Craig Roberts:

The Walking Dead: A Marine's Story of Vietnam (Pocket Books with Charles W. Sasser)

One Shot—One Kill: America's Combat Snipers from WWII to Beirut (Pocket Books with Charles W. Sasser)

Combat Medic—Vietnam (Pocket Books)

Police Sniper (Pocket Books)

Crosshairs on the Kill Zone (Pocket Books with Charles W. Sasser)

Kill Zone: A Sniper Looks at Dealey Plaza (Consolidated Press Int'l)

The Medusa File: Crimes and Coverups of the U.S. Government (Consolidated Press Int'l)

JFK: The Dead Witnesses (Consolidated Press Int'l)

The Hind Heist (Consolidated Press Int'l)

The Dragunov Solution (Consolidated Press Int'l)

Hell Hound (Avon, with Allen Appel)

Desert Storm (Contributing author with Harry Summers, Empire Press)

The New Face of War (Contributing writer for Time-Life books)